DRONE

Cover designed by W. M. J. Kreucher

This book is a work of fiction. Names, characters, places, and incidents either are products of the author's imagination or used fictitiously. Any resemblance to actual persons, living or dead, events, or locales is entirely coincidental.

W. M. J. Kreucher
Visit my website at walt.kreucher.net

Printed in the United States of America

First Printing: June 2014
Second Printing 2016
Third Printing 2017

Dandelion Man Press

ISBN-979-8-8693-3968-3

This novel is dedicated to my classmates.

"*One day you will ask me which is more important? My life or yours? I will say mine and you will walk away not knowing that you are my life.*"

—KAHLIL GIBRAN

ACKNOWLEDGEMENTS

I want to acknowledge my friends and colleagues. They know who they are. I have borrowed liberally from their character traits in writing this manuscript. Thank you for the loan of your personas.

INTRODUCTION

We have all read the internet stories of individual so-called 'experts' who have developed smart-phone apps that would allow them to take over a commercial airliner. This story takes that possibility one step further.

CHAPTER 1

May 15th

VASILI GRIGORY KONSTANTINOV WAS, by any standard, a solitary man, a quiet man. This was the main reason he had remained single, though if he was completely honest with himself, there were other reasons. His employer saw fit to have him travel the world conducting business.

Vasili was, in fact, the perfect company man. He had lived in several countries, spoke five languages, and took a personal interest in international affairs. He traveled the world and toiled in relative obscurity. Today he was in Kiev, a city he had been to before.

Kiev was alive with activity. On the Dnieper River, it was a majestic capital city, home to some three million people. One of the oldest cities in Eastern Europe, adorned with Orthodox Cathedrals and palaces. Centuries old structures and modern architectural masterpieces dotted the cityscape as the old and new mixed naturally. Over the generations, for as long as anyone could remember, the city had changed national allegiances many times. At one point, it belonged to Lithuania. Poland took it over for a while, and then Russia before the city and the entire

Ukraine declared its independence after World War I. Since that time, it was usurped by the Soviet Union after the Second World War, then became independent again when the Soviet Union broke up. The last one hundred years had been an on-again, off-again relationship with its eastern neighbor.

The city itself was an important industrial, financial, and technology center. Many important businesses had offices in the city center. While those in business tried to maintain some sense of normalcy, the increasing animosity between the Pro-Russian and Pro-Ukraine factions was growing by the day. Fights were breaking out on the streets and even in homes. Everyone, it seemed, had an opinion and loudly voiced that opinion on rejoining the Russian Federation or remaining independent.

Vasili had been living in a nondescript company provided flat in the Old Town section for the past month. No one ever noticed him or asked for his opinion.

The spartan flat had a double bed, a simple wood desk with a single chair; a dresser with five drawers. The bare gray-green walls reminded him of the halls leading to his uncle's office. It was more of a staging area than a place to live. It suited Vasili's purpose and allowed him to make his arrangements and conduct his affairs in quiet solitude.

Today had started like any other since he had arrived. Vasili got up early. He went downstairs and across the street to the diner and ordered breakfast. He sat quietly, reading the morning paper as he waited for his order to be filled. The front page had an article on a fire the night before, but the headline story was about the special session of Parliament that was to take place later that day. The national leaders wanted to enter the debate that was welling up in the streets. Vasili couldn't help but chuckle at the elegant prose the editorial staff had prepared, outlining what steps Parliament needed to take and in what order. Everything specified logically.

As he finished his breakfast, he eavesdropped on conversations around him. The topics tended mostly to business, though some involved family matters. The man in the old brown coat sitting at the counter was flirting with the waitress, trying for what seemed like the umpteenth time to get a phone number from her. She smiled sweetly when she noticed Vasili watching them flirt, then she moved on to pour some coffee for another customer and bring a piece of pie to the man two stools away. No one that morning seemed to be interested in the workings of the government, or in the meeting that was to take place that very morning. What the politicians thought meant nothing to their meager lives.

Today was to be his last day in Kiev. He was scheduled to leave town on another assignment. He was always needed, first here; then there. Nowhere could he call home anymore. He had lived out of a suitcase most of his life, so much so that he could hardly remember a time when he had a home.

After breakfast, he took a paper cup of coffee with him as he walked out into the brisk morning air, pulling his wool coat tight against his neck, the wind blowing his dark hair wildly as it swirled in the cavernous corridor of buildings. He walked to his car and drove across town.

When he reached the office, he took the elevator to the twelfth floor and exited. He was alone at that early morning hour, only his cup of coffee for a friend. Vasili had only one appointment that morning and that was with Matviyko Sliva, the Chairman of the Ukrainian Parliament. Sliva was a hawk and was dead set against Ukraine rejoining Russia. The meeting wasn't for another hour and a half, so Vasili would have plenty of time to get everything ready.

He sat by the window, gazing out at the clouds that were gathering. They were moving in a south-easterly direction at about ten kilometers per hour; he estimated. Not ideal conditions, but not out of the ordinary; nothing he hadn't seen in the past. He combed his hair with his fingers, trying to get it into order after the wind on the street had tossed it to and fro.

Vasili had taken off his coat and laid it across a chair in the corner of the office. The hot coffee was a guilty pleasure. He had never needed caffeine in the morning, especially on a day such as this, but he enjoyed the aroma, the taste on his lips, and the blackness of its color.

As the time for his meeting approached, he went over to his coat and began unzipping the compartments. He pulled out several white plastic pieces, and when everything was on the floor in front of him, he began assembling the Dragunov. When it was ready, he loaded the magazine with the three bullets he carried in his pocket. He only needed one, but his Uncle Dmitri had always insisted that he carry two backup bullets as a contingency.

When the motorcade carrying Sliva stopped across the street, Vasili was already in position. Sliva was a large man with a healthy appetite. That meant that as he swung his legs out of the back seat of the black Mercedes limousine, he would pause ever so slightly before lifting himself off the seat. In that momentary pause, the shot rang out. The reverberation of the noise in the canyon of buildings made it impossible to pinpoint the location.

Vasili knew it was a kill even before the security detail did. Never once did he think if the man had any family. He calmly withdrew the barrel from the window, closed it, disassembled the weapon, and slipped the pieces back into the zippered compartments of his coat.

DRONE

As he rode down the elevator, he had one hand in his pocket; the other holding the cup of coffee. None of the other passengers paid him any attention. They were all engrossed in their morning routine, rushing off to meetings, engaging in conversations with associates, sniffing the intoxicating scent of perfume wafting from secretaries. No one seemed to know what had happened on the street outside, and no one noticed the man in the dark coat who seemed in no particular hurry.

As Vasili walked out of the building, he purposely stopped himself from looking down the street to the motorcade. He wanted to admire his work, but his training forbid him from doing that. He turned and then walked away from the action as if he hadn't a care in the world. It would be up to others to deal with the repercussions.

His uncle had ordered the kill. It sent a message. Sliva was important enough that his assassination would garner worldwide attention, but not so important as to bring down any international sanctions. Besides, who would they sanction?

CHAPTER 2

SAM KENNEDY WAS A GENIUS, a freaking genius. You could tell just by looking at him. One look was all it took. Take him out of the affluent suburb where he lived, dress him in Salvation Army remnants, place him downtown in the Cass Corridor, and people would still say that he was a genius. He had that look about him.

Not that he was handsome. No one had ever saddled him with that label. No, on the contrary, he was plain, even average looking, with thinning hair and eyes that were more gray than blue.

If he had a flaw, it was his irritating generosity; that generosity compelled him to give too much to charity, too much to the Catholic Church, too much to his damn high school. Couldn't he once in a while buy Helen a new dress, like the red one trimmed with black and white that she saw in the mall at White House–Black Market? Not that Helen needed Sam to buy things for her. After all, she had worked for almost forty years herself and together; they had built a wonderful life. Nor was she ungrateful for those gifts Sam gave her. God knows she loved that man. It's just that she wanted—no, needed—attention once in a while. And now she needed him to agree to travel the world with her.

DRONE

* * *

Sam was finishing penning a note to his wife. Helen had gone to bed early that evening. Sam stayed downstairs under the pretense of having to finish some work.

My Dearest Friend,

It is with great fondness that I call to mind the first time I lay beside you. Even then, I couldn't help but reach over and touch your hand as we lay together, side-by-side. I'm certain you remember it as well as I do. The smell of tempera paints and paste in the air. Mrs. Boil pacing back and forth across the front of the kindergarten class as we all took our nap.

You were the first friend I made at school and you are still my best friend.

I can't believe we have been together these fifty-five plus years, the last thirty-eight as man and wife. I have been so fortunate to have found you so early and that you have stayed by my side for so long.

Thank you

With all my love,

Sam

P.S. Happy Anniversary.

The letter Sam prepared that evening was only a small part of the preparations he was making for the following day. He left the letter on the place mat on the breakfast table, which was a glass-top affair with a bluish-green wrought iron frame and chairs. The table fit well with the royal cherry cabinets and an off-white ceramic tile floor. Helen always sat next to Sam at meal time. Her chair was adjacent to the bay window that looked out into the garden. In the spring, orioles would come, and feed

13

from the grape jam she would leave in a small cup placed atop the bird feeder.

Sam had also left a card on the nightstand beside Helen's bed. After penning the note, he brought out the dozen white roses he had purchased earlier in the day, placed them in a cut-glass vase, and left them on the granite island in the kitchen, where she would be sure to see them. They were by no means an elaborate gift, but they were heartfelt.

In the days preceding their anniversary, Helen had retired from her job, working first as a nurse and later as a hospital administrator. This was to be the first anniversary when one of them was no longer working. Sam had wanted to retire too, but the finances didn't add up in his mind. He would continue working part time from home, writing computer code for whomever would hire him.

It was always Helen's dream to travel the world, visit Paris in the spring, walk along the Danube in autumn, even stay in a castle in Ireland. Sam was the opposite. He wanted to spend his retirement years at home, living comfortably, reading and watching the grass grow in his backyard. Far too many hours had he spent on the tarmac waiting out yet another delay; too many hours stuck in rush hour traffic in some god-forsaken downtown in another city that looked like the last one he was in. But that was the nature of contract work. He went where the jobs were.

The home they shared was in a small suburb west of Detroit. It was a modern ranch decorated in off-white. The home immediately signaled there were no children living there.

The neighborhood consisted mostly of brick ranches with some colonials mixed in. Their home was but a few blocks from downtown, a pleasant walkable district with kitschy shops and an excellent selection of restaurants. Often in the evening, they would walk downtown when the weather was nice. The people were all friendly and everyone seemed to know everyone.

It was a mixed community, some young couples starting families and some older folks that had already retired and were looking forward to spoiling their grandkids. Sam and Helen had no children, and that meant no grandchildren to spoil. It's not that they didn't try; it was just one of those things that never worked out. They would have to find something else to do in retirement.

According to his calculations on his longevity and Helen's, and factoring in their bank accounts, he would have to work another six years. Only then would he have a sufficient cushion to make that fateful decision and retire. It made him break out in a cold sweat every time he thought about the prospect of retiring.

Sam had been a computer programmer for as long as he could remember. Until a few years ago, when the recession hit, he had worked for one of the auto companies. He was in that now infamous meeting where the Senior Vice President had proclaimed, after looking around the room, "we have too many old white guys here."

Not long after that, the company gave Sam a 'voluntary' retirement package. He always thought he was too young to retire. When you are white, over fifty and male, it is impossible to find regular employment. So, he went into business for himself, working from his home. The pay was less, and sometimes the hours; but the commute from the kitchen to the den was a breeze. That part he liked.

The projects he worked on varied with the clients. He did work for the government, for the Department of Defense, on software revisions. He worked for the phone company on switching software for their mainframes.

He was bright and a quick study, with a knack for looking at a set of code and knowing exactly how to improve it or to fix some problem that the company was having. It was a gift, though sometimes it was also a curse as he would lose himself in the code fixing problems created by others that were not a part of the original contract. Sam always found one more thing he wanted to take care of before he could let go of the project.

His clients loved the fact that he always delivered more than he'd promised and was always on time or ahead of schedule. He was the best in the world at what he did, not that anyone ever noticed or cared.

After Sam arranged the flowers and set the letter against the clear, cut-glass vase, he turned out the lights and walked up the stairs to join his wife in bed.

CHAPTER 3

THE INTERNATIONAL PUSHBACK FROM THE assassination was predictable, but short-lived. It was over even before Vasili had reached Moscow. He had hired a car in Kiev and left it at the border, where a 'company' driver picked him up after he crossed the border.

Though he was not a fan of the high-tech plastic weapons made with those new-fangled three-dimensional printers, they came in handy when you had to cross a border or travel by airplane. His preferred weapon was the Makarov pistol he carried. It was the only reminder he had of his parents.

In the days that followed, Vasili met with Uncle Dmitri. He was never really sure that the man was his biological uncle, but for as long as he could remember, he called the man by that name. Dmitri had taken care of him when he was young, then sent Vasili to a series of well-structured foster homes, sometimes in Bulgaria, sometimes in Germany. He even once lived with a family in the United States. The boy had a quick ear for language and a fertile mind.

"Excellent work, my boy." Uncle Dmitri was never one to be overly extravagant in his praise, but the little he provided meant a great deal to the man.

Vasili nodded, not smiling or even looking at his uncle.

"I have another assignment for you. I want you to go on my behalf to meet with the Resistance in Syria. They are badly in need of material goods in their quest to establish the peaceful Caliphate el-Lavant. We must help in this humanitarian effort. Take a few days off, then you can travel as you wish. The details are in the encrypted file I just sent to you. You will be alone on this trip. We need to keep it under the radar, and I know I can trust your discretion. We will use the usual route shipping the goods once all the arrangements are finalized. Your fee for this one will be the usual one percent plus an additional six percent for war zone pay and I have provided a three percent bonus, because I like you."

Vasili nodded his agreement and left his uncle's office. It would be a long time before he would see that face again.

* * *

When Vasili arrived in Azaz, word quickly spread among the Resistance and the leadership of Jaish al-Muhajireen cheered him as a savior. He was nothing of the sort, and he demanded that those he met with close off any communication with the rest of their group until after his departure, or he would immediately return to neutral territory. Word was not to leak out that he was there on business.

Of course, the Resistance complied with his request. They had no choice. They needed his goods more than Vasili needed their money.

When they first met at the coordinates provided in the encrypted file, his hosts did not expect his Western accent. They had expected something completely different. Vasili smiled at their stupidity. *Idiots*, he thought.

Over the next several days, the discussion languished. The Resistance demanding this or that. Vasili nodded occasionally. More often, he shook his head. There was only so much support he could provide. Vasili used the time to learn as much as he could about the group. Inevitably, the discussion turned to the subject of drones, those unmanned aerial vehicles that were spying on their positions and targeting weapons stockpiles. Drones could sweep in almost unknown because of their size and destroy millions of dollars of material with a single missile shot. The operator could be thousands of miles away, relaying commands via satellite links and still be home for dinner with his family. The Resistance demanded such capability. They were tired of crawling on their bellies for the scraps of dirt they controlled, only to be pushed back by a single unmanned drone. They wanted to change the face of war forever.

Vasili patiently listened to their ranting, zealous fervor, their plea that even Allāh demanded that he provide these tools. The pleas fell on deaf ears. Though raised a Christian, and was even Catholic, once, religion was all muddled up in his mind. His theological trinity was fostering discord, unrest, and chaos.

From time to time, he sipped the qahwa, though the hot beverage only enhanced the heat that reflected off the walls and ceiling of the tent. He never quite got used to the heat, though he had spent a year in Arabia after Cambridge. He wasn't always listening to the demands being presented to him. Often his mind wandered, always thinking and listening to the side conversations that were taking place in Farsi. When the group finished with their lengthy listing of material goods and assistance, Vasili held up his hand, as if to stop any further conversation. He pulled out a slip of paper from his left shirt pocket and handed it to al-Marica. It contained the total of what he would provide, Swedish carbines, Chinese rocket launchers, and German rocket-propelled grenades. At the bottom was a price tag. There was to be no negotiation.

Though outnumbered seven to one, he was confident that if it came to a contest, he would be the only man to leave the tent.

Al-Marcia nodded and passed over the metal container with the diamonds. Vasili didn't need to count them or even examine them. Everyone knew that any shortage would mean certain death.

Vasili handed over a second slip of paper with the access codes to the shipping company's dispatch offices and the arrangements were complete. The Resistance would order the goods whenever they wanted and have them delivered; however, they wanted. It was no longer Vasili's concern.

He thanked his hosts for their hospitality and departed the same way he had come.

CHAPTER 4

PAT O'CONNOR WAS BY ALL ACCOUNTS the cheerful, upbeat sort. He lived a peaceful existence with his significant other in a brick two-story home in Pontiac. Nothing important had ever happened in the quiet neighborhood where the house stood. Like all the other houses nearby, it had been built in the nineteen twenties and kept most of the flavor of that bygone era. Jamie saw to that.

She had an artist's touch and worked as a graphic artist in downtown Birmingham. On the weekends, she would follow Pat to whatever Irish bar he was playing at and sip a Killian's Red while doing her sketching while Pat sang melodies of the old country. He was particularly in demand during the St. Patrick's Day festivities.

Jamie was tall, which suited Pat, and slim. One could call her skinny. She was not anorexic, thin, nor sickly. She was just tall and very, very thin. Jamie was no pushover. She wore the pants in their little family and kept Pat in line. He didn't mind. It was nice to have someone care about him after all those years.

After their evening meal, Pat would clear the table and put the dishes into the dishwasher. It was mindless work, and he enjoyed the simple task after a long day working in the office. Anything that would recenter his thinking.

"Do you have a gig this weekend?" Jamie asked.

"Nope. Got the reunion."

"Reunion? What reunion?"

"Forty-fifth high school reunion."

"You're not going to that, are you? I can hardly remember what school I graduated from, let alone go back and relive that experience."

Pat laughed at Jamie's description of her high school years. His recollection was far different. "I have fond memories of high school, you know that."

"I don't have to go, do I?" Jamie wasn't interested in hearing the old stories one more time.

"No, there will be no significant others. Just the guys."

"Friday or Saturday?"

"Both actually, Friday is the stag night at the school and Saturday we go out and commit golf at Tanglewood." Pat spoke the last part of the sentence in a mock Scottish accent.

"You don't play golf." Jamie played and never once did Pat offer to join her for a round. He didn't even own a set of clubs.

"No one really plays golf. Though the way we play it, it's more of a crime."

Jamie shook her head and smiled. By now, she was used to the quirkiness that was her friend.

Pat finished stacking the dishes in the dishwasher and moved on to cleaning the pots.

"You have any plans?" He asked mindlessly as he ran the pot under the hot water, rinsing off the soap.

"Me? No, not really. I thought I would paint some. I need the release. It's been such a hard week." Jamie looked up for a moment, then glanced out the window into the night. There was no movement in the darkness of their yard, and the stillness of the night was a comfort. She went back to reading the evening news on her tablet. The evening was a time for her to decompress; a time to allow the cares of the day to drift away and to recharge her batteries for the coming day.

In the time she had known Pat, they had grown together, though each kept their separate interests. Pat had his love of music, Jamie her love of art and painting. To be sure, they enjoyed each other's passion for their craft and genuinely appreciated the gift the other possessed. They had found each other late in life and were content with what they had. More than content. They loved each other. Theirs was a love born of maturity, not the silly, romantic love of youth with its meaningless gestures and emotional outbursts. It was as deep as an ocean and as quiet as a calm sea on a moonlight night.

Pat finished the dishes, went off to the living room and picked up his guitar. He played the lively, if bawdy, Irish drinking songs that were so popular at the gigs he did on weekends: Seven Drunken Nights, The German Clockwinder, All for Me Grog and many others. By ten o'clock, it was time to shift gears. The bawdiness of the melodies gave way to more melancholy, quieter tunes. The relaxing notes put one in the mood for a restful night. Even that eventually gave way as he put down the guitar and turned on the old turntable he kept in working order. Tonight, he put on a vinyl disk with the soulful music of the San Sebastian Strings and the poetic readings of Rod McKuen.

During the week, Pat worked for the Department of Natural Resources as a biologist who specialized in aquatic life. He was an expert on everything from algae to zebra mussels. If it lived or grew in the water, he knew about it and how to make it survive and thrive.

His current interest was in isolating particular strains of micro-algae that would contribute to higher yields when converted into synthetic motor fuel. These fast-growing organisms had the potential, he thought, of eventually replacing all fossil fuels. Part of his job with the Department of Natural Resources required him to go to ponds and stagnant water pools around the state to assess and catalog the growth and strain of algae. He knew every type of strain there was, which ones were harmless, and which ones were toxic to plants and animals. He knew how to promote their growth to foster those strains that were beneficial, and how to curtail the growth of those strains that presented a hazard. It was enjoyable work that fostered his love of the environment and allowed him to get plenty of fresh air on those days when he was in the field.

CHAPTER 5

DMITRI WAS SITTING BEHIND HIS LARGE wooden desk in his corner office in the Lubyanka Building, a century-old structure just off the square, when the phone rang.

"Yes?"

"It is done," was all the voice said. A click could be heard on the other end.

"Who was that?" Miesha asked.

"Vasili. He did a favor for me."

"I don't know why you continue to trust that man. If it were up to me, I would put him in the basement." Miesha shook his head as he got up from his leather wing chair and walked over to the window. A trail of smoke from his cigar followed like the vapor trail of some airplane high in the firmament.

"Don't be so hard on the boy. He comes from excellent stock. Did you know his parents were the first heroes of our beloved country?"

"Is that why you take a special interest in him?" Miesha was not interested, but it didn't pay to offend Dmitri.

"Partly. He was orphaned at the age of three when an American spy gunned down his parents in cold blood. I often suspected that he witnessed the killing, but could never confirm this. He denies it, of course, or at least denies remembering

25

anything." Dmitri wrote out a note that he would add to the file later.

"I still don't trust the man. He is too much of a loner. A man of solitude exposes himself to certain psychological dangers. You know that as well as I."

"Perhaps. But he has his uses. He is the best in the world at what he does. He accepts assignments no other agent would dare tackle alone. Never once has he failed to complete a mission." The thought of Vasili's prowess in the field was a source of great pride to Dmitri.

"I can't argue with his success. What have we for his next action?"

"I have given him an assignment in Berlin. We are revising our monitoring capability, and I need him to oversee the last steps. His presence will emphasize the importance of secrecy lest we have an unfortunate incident such as our friends in America had with our guest, Edward. So much has changed since we duplicated the 'five eyes' network, Miesha. The world has changed in ways no one could have predicted. Without knowing it, many ignorant Americans are simply giving away national secrets on their social media. It makes our job much easier. We need to keep up with the times and enhance the system's ability to sift the wheat from the chaff."

"And Brussels, London, and Paris?"

"Yes, yes, enhancements are already underway. But it is the Americas that are the largest gold mine of information. We have our experts' planting code that will undermine their abilities and provide us with what we need. I miss those days when we actually worked the field, when agents were agents. We are a dying breed, Miesha. Soon, there will no longer be a need for our type. Computer experts will do everything, I'm afraid. But not

Vasili. He has found a place that few can fill. There will always be a need for him."

* * *

Vasili's cut from the Resistance affair made him a wealthy man, not that he ever counted his money. It appeared in numbered accounts in banks around the world. He withdrew cash as he saw fit. His was a simple life most of the time.

Berlin was a town that suited his lifestyle. The nightlife was eclectic. It was one of the few places in the world where you tipped your waiter with a glass of beer. Everyone drank heartily.

"Are you certain?" Vasili asked, leaning over the security officer's shoulder. He examined the screen but couldn't make heads or tails of the commands that were streaming across the screen.

"Pretty much." The reply was almost apologetic as the man pointed to a string of code that showed the operator who had accessed the file last.

"Who else had access?" Vasili questioned the security technician.

"No one in the last forty-eight hours."

Vasili didn't need any additional information. He walked out of the security office and down to the second floor, where the contract employees were all busily writing code and sifting through mock intelligence data intermixed with random chatter. A juicy tidbit of planted intelligence had proved too tempting to one tech who thought himself a bit too clever.

Vasili tapped the technician on the shoulder. "Come with me."

The others looked up to see who dared come into the room that was supposed to be for classified workers only. When they saw the look on Vasili's face, every technician immediately put his head down and began banging away on the keys faster than ever.

"Wait, what did I do?" The startled look on his face betrayed the knowledge of why he was being singled out.

"Come."

There was to be no further explanation. When the two people were out the door, Vasili grabbed the twenty-something tech by the arm and hustled him out the back of the building and into a waiting car. The strength of Vasili's grip startled the young technician. He struggled to pull himself free, twisting and turning, but it was to no avail. With his free arm, Vasili opened the passenger door of the car and pushed the young man down into the seat.

"If you run, I will kill you on the street." The simple command was all that was said. Vasili walked to the driver's side and took his place. The man beside him didn't move.

"Where are we going? Can you at least tell me what I did? Here, you can have the file. It is nothing, nothing really. Understand? I needed the money for my mother. She is dying. We have no money for a doctor. You must say something." The frantic tone in the technician's voice had an irritatingly high pitch.

Out on the autobahn, about a hundred and eleven kilometers from the city center, the car pulled to a stop at the farthest end of an unmanaged rest area. The area was small and deserted, as the Raststätte was only a few kilometers further. Vasili pushed the body out the door. He never even bothered to check the pockets to collect the data file. There was no need.

DRONE

Vasili pulled the car back onto the road and pointed it toward Brussels.

CHAPTER 6

IT WAS SEVEN O'CLOCK IN THE EVENING, the scheduled starting time, and already there were almost a dozen cars in the parking lot outside the door where the sign read 'reunion'. Pat pulled into a parking spot and walked inside. Gathered around the sign-in table were old friends. Yearbooks from the four years they had walked those hallowed halls—maybe not these halls—were sitting on the tables. The school Pat knew so well had been torn down a few years earlier. The new building stood on fresh land a few miles from the old site. It was a state-of-the-art facility, complete with white boards linked to the school's network of computers. Teachers could have interactive lectures that used slides projected onto the boards. The heavy backpacks the students hauled from class to class in the old days were now replaced with iPad tablets that were preloaded with all the books the students would need. Teachers emailed students their assignments; tests were taken digitally. It was a different world, one that was foreign to students in the sixties.

The school had been a paragon of middle-class values and work ethic. Sure, there were a few who were from wealth, but wealth meant little once they entered those halls. What mattered was the character of the individual and the friendship they shared.

"Pat, you old dog. How've you been?" Mike said, leaning with one hand on his walker. He extended his other hand in a warm handshake.

"Mike? Is that you? What happened?" Pat asked, looking at the man who was once so robust.

Mike had been an Army Ranger during Vietnam and had spent many a night sleeping on the wet jungle floor during his tour of duty. He never complained; he did it out of a sense of duty to his country.

"Knees have finally given out—osteoarthritis—hips too. But I get around. Just need a bit of help when I have to stand for long periods."

The faces in the crowd were mostly recognizable, though many were now buried beneath white hair; that is if there was any hair left.

"I see Sam is here already and Larry."

Pat and Mike moved closer together as Larry snapped a photo with his smartphone.

"I'm documenting the class for the website." Larry said by way of explanation.

Around the cafeteria, where they gathered for the evening festivities, the classmates were congregating in small groups of three or four, reliving the old days, repeating favorite stories, and updating each other on the path their lives had taken. There was very little pretense in this room, in this group. Everyone knew most of the secrets, even the ones they told no one else. Somehow, word always got around, though no one shared the secrets with outsiders.

Sam walked over and joined Pat and Mike in pointing at the walker. Like most of the classmates, he was shocked to see a walker being used so early in the life of someone his own age. There was no malice or disrespect intended.

"Old war wound?" The tone of concern for a friend reverberated in Sam's voice.

"Partially. I don't think the years in Nam did them much good, but the VA says it's not service related so they won't pay to have the knees rebuilt. I just have to make do." Mike shrugged as he leaned his body on the handles of his walker, taking some of the weight off the knees.

"Those were tough years." Gerry said, joining the group. He was sporting a long ponytail reminiscent of the sixties. Back in high school, the head disciplinarian forbad hair that touch the collar of your shirt or hung down covering your eyes. It meant certain JUG (Justice Under God) after school and a trip to see Mr. Sharp for a free haircut. Over the years, many rebelled against those rigid restrictions after they left school. Some were still rebelling.

"I still remember my draft number, two hundred twenty-two. It was just above the call up level that year. I was lucky. Sorry Mike." Gerry hadn't served his country in Viet Nam or any other war. He used his student deferment until the war ended. That didn't mean he disrespected those who wanted to serve or had been drafted into the service. He had great respect for Mike and the others from the class that had chosen that route.

"Hey, I did what I had to do. I wasn't about to retreat to Canada like some. My draft number was single digits. I knew the night they drew the numbers that I would be in the first group called up, so I enlisted. At least that way I got to choose the branch and the timing."

"It must have been difficult. I can't imagine that kind of life. I don't know if I could do it." Gerry continued.

Mike shrugged. "We did what we did. Most of the time, it wasn't bad. I spent my fair share of time crawling on my belly through swampland. And if the 'Op Ranch Handers' weren't careful or if the wind changed direction suddenly, you could get a face full of Agent. Not a pleasant aroma."

Pat shook his head. He was familiar with biotoxins in his fieldwork and knew well the dangers of Agent Orange.

"Now they do it all by remote control." Larry offered. "They operate from half a world away looking at computer screens."

"Don't know if that's better or worse. You can't look into the eyes of the man you are killing. But then, chemical warfare wasn't the most moral route to take either. I never understood what the brass was thinking. We did what we were told and followed orders." Mike never felt the need to defend the Army.

"I read the other day that drones were the new weapon of choice. They were being deployed for all sorts of things, assassinations, spying, even border security. Some uses seem reasonable. I'm not sure about all of them." Sam offered.

"And who's to say they are secure? Couldn't anyone steal one?" Gerry asked.

"I don't think so." Mike rejoined the conversation, wrinkling up his face as if to express his skepticism.

"I'm not so sure. I read an article a year ago about a man who developed an app for a smartphone that allowed him to commandeer a commercial airliner. It seems a drone would be easy once you got through the security firewall." Sam began thinking through the steps in his mind. His brain was always working.

"Go on. Couldn't happen. The operator on the ground would know the second he lost control. He probably has a self-destruct mechanism that would trigger." Mike knew enough about military tactics that there had to be some failsafe.

"Not necessarily. You would have to spoof the signals back to the original operator and maybe even spoof the video feed, but that wouldn't be impossible, especially for a drone that routinely flew similar missions. The operator might not know for sure until the drone was due to return to base for refueling or deviated from the routine flight path." Larry interjected.

"You can't hack into the DoD computers to get the software. Those have to be the most secure computers on the planet," Gerry argued.

"You may not have to. NASA and ICE use the drones for various civilian operations, and I've heard some police departments are considering using them. It would be easier and less risky to hack into one of those systems to get the basic command software." Sam pointed out. He wasn't an expert on that sort of thing. It just seemed like a logical path for a criminal mind.

"And you don't think the FBI would be on your tail in a few days?" Mike couldn't help but defend the security of the country.

"Maybe. But if you used a series of burner laptops, say laptops purchased in Dearborn from Craigslist, you could point them toward Middle Eastern Terrorist groups. It would throw the feds off your trail for a while."

Everyone's eyebrows lifted as they turned to Tom Parker, a former Michigan state trooper who had joined the conversation.

"Not a bad idea. You would make an evil terrorist." Gerry quipped.

Everyone laughed at the absurdity of the comment.

"What would you use as a weapon's kit? That would be more difficult to come by. The military probably guards the missiles much more carefully, at least I hope they do."

"A terrorist could get missiles overseas from any number of places."

"Thinking outside the box, couldn't you convert one of the fuel tanks to a holding tank for a chemical weapon?" Pat suggested, following up on Mike's earlier comment on Agent Orange.

"Where would you get something like that?" Mike looked at him quizzically.

"Most any pond in the area has algae in it. Some of that stuff is pretty toxic. You could easily take some pond scum, put it under some fluorescent lamps for a few days to concentrate it and you would have the makings for a deadly aerosol. Some toxins are more powerful than the nerve gas used in World War II." Pat responded. "Hey, I'm not suggesting it. Just thinking out loud." He held up his hands as if to plead his innocence.

The group nodded at the completeness of their plan. In only a few minutes, they took over the world.

CHAPTER 7

BRUSSELS WAS A SIMPLE ASSIGNMENT. Vasili just had to show up at the operation task force location and walk through the area. Word had already spread across the network about the missing Berlin tech, the menacing man who had been in the building. The one who had escorted the tech out. No one dared to look up at Vasili as he walked through the rows of computers sitting side-by-side on long tables, three or four operators at a table. No one needed to be reminded of the penalty for trying to steal state secrets and sell them for a profit. Their hands shook as they tried to type faster, their palms sweating, staining the keyboards with the oil and dirt from their fingers. Machiavellian order had been established through a simple drive down the autobahn.

There would be little need to go to Paris or London. The seeds had all been planted. Tomorrow he would listen in on the chatter. It might prove comical to see what the new world order offered.

Word around the water cooler was that the stranger was also responsible for the killing in Kiev. Some were skeptical. Others insisted this was the man responsible, or at least someone like him. They spoke in hushed tones, the speaker always looking over his shoulder to see who might be listening. No one wanted to be the next one to take a ride out of town.

Whenever Vasili came into a room, it was the same. No one spoke to him or even looked in his direction. That was the life he had made for himself. But then, he was used to the solitude.

When he was a boy, after his parents died, he lived on the streets. Garbage was his daily sustenance. The first few times he had stolen a piece of fruit from a street vendor, he got caught and beaten severely. It didn't take him long to become adept at theft. As he grew, he joined gangs of other homeless youth. He never found them particularly useful. The hierarchical structure didn't suit his appetite. He had no respect for authority. The experience taught him how to fight, how to beat a boy twice his size. His was a toughness and a lust for violence that few dared match. Even the leaders gave him a wide berth, fearful that one day he would challenge them. Not that he was ever interested in running an operation. He stole only what he needed to survive and gave nothing away.

There was a single bundle that he always carried. In the early years, it looked bigger than he was, and almost as heavy. As he grew, it became a part of him, always tucked in his pants behind his back, within easy reach. Occasionally, he would steal a bullet from a police officer's belt. His preference was not to use the weapon. It was to get things through a menacing look or a swift hand.

It was when he was ten or twelve that he met Dmitri. Vasili had made his way to Bulgaria by then and was making a comfortable living in Sofia. The conditions were ripe for a lad with his talents. He had picked Dmitri's pocket one afternoon as his future mentor was wandering through the tents of the bazaar looking for a set of Matryoshka dolls for his young niece.

Dmitri, of course, didn't know someone had picked his pocket until he went to pay for the hand-carved stacking dolls he had selected. He chuckled that some young urchin had claimed him as a victim. It was a mistake few dared to make.

Dmitri came back to the market each day for the next two weeks, studying the crowd, watching the various thieves ply their trade. It was not until he had seen and dismissed Vasili several times that he finally caught him in the act. This was a supreme master thief, he thought.

Dmitri grabbed Vasili by the collar and gave him a look that would freeze a grown man. Vasili glared right back, as if he would burn a hole through the man holding him.

"I see you have skills and you have no fear. That is good. But you must learn discipline."

Vasili twisted his body and in a flash, he had escaped the grasp of Dmitri.

"I mean you no harm. You misunderstand my intentions." Dmitri offered in a soft voice, like one would use with a favorite nephew.

The crowd that had gathered to assist the young boy now took a step back as they saw who was speaking. They had seen his type before, and even the gypsies were not stupid enough to challenge them. The Bulgarian Secret Police were well known for their 'special power' to make people disappear.

The hushed crowd now pressed together, preventing Vasili from escaping.

"Come, walk with me. We have much to discuss." The tone in Dmitri's voice was calming, not at all agitated, as Vasili had expected. Something inside of him told him that this man meant him no harm. Indeed, he reminded him of someone from his distant past.

38

CHAPTER 8

AT SIX THIRTY SATURDAY MORNING, the sun was peeking its rosy head over the horizon and the mist was wafting up from the grass. The first cars were already entering the parking lot. Slowly, the classmates arrived, some alone in their cars, others came in pairs. Most had a cup of coffee in their hands.

They sat on the bumpers of their car as they removed their shoes and replaced them with their golf spikes. Caps were placed on the heads, sunglasses tucked safely away in a pocket in the event the sun came out later. Then the slow march of the clubs made their way on the backs of the golfers into the Pro Shop, where the group would pay the green fees for the morning round of golf.

It was easiest to get a block of tee times first thing in the morning. There would be no one on the tee ahead of them, so they could be assured of a quick round if that was what they wanted.

Not everyone in the group was skilled at the game. Indeed, golf is the type of game that can never be perfected, only enjoyed, even when you are cursing the ball for not going in the direction you intended.

The group agreed in advance that a simple scramble format would suffice for the day. That way, each team could optimize the best shot and they could pick the duffs up so as not to slow down the rest of the golfers.

One member from the organizing committee had previously arranged the golfers into foursomes. Everyone knew everyone else, so there was no need for introductions. Most of the classmates still lived in the state, though many traveled thousands of miles for this weekend adventure. They played together once every five years, and it didn't matter who played with whom.

Two by two, the golfers got into their carts and started the parade to the first tee. The first tee at dawn, with the mist rising from the fairway, was a beautiful sight to any golfer. It was especially pleasing to a group of old friends, enjoying a shared activity.

As the first ball was struck, the laughter and the joking were already well underway. No one was above a bit of good-natured ribbing in a group such as this, though many also offered constructive coaching to those who needed a flaw corrected or simply wanted a free lesson. It was a friendly game, one they all looked forward to.

After the round, the group met in the clubhouse for lunch and a bit of score deflating.

There were the awards for closest to the pin, longest drive and other festivities that occupied those already seated as the last of the group made their way to the dining area. The lunch conversation inevitably returned to memories of teachers and high school events. It was a continuation of the conversations from the previous night in the cafeteria. There were almost as many individuals who showed up for lunch as those who played the round of golf in the morning, even a few who could not make the Friday night activity.

"I ran into Father Paramo the other day." Gerry said as he came up to Sam.

"He was my favorite teacher in high school. He taught me how to solve problems." Sam's admiration for his former teacher continued long after he left high school.

"Were you in his class the day Tom's back seat caught fire?" Gerry asked.

"Yeah, the entire class raced to the window. Boy, was Tom mad when he found out Tim had dropped his cigarette down behind the seat." The memory brought a smile to Sam's face.

"The entire school was watching when the fire trucks came. I didn't want to be in Tim's shoes when Tom caught up with him after school."

After golf, the guys pushed several tables together in the dining area so that everyone could sit in close proximity at one long table that extended the width of the room. The view looking out of the window was that of a gazebo and a water fountain centered in a pond behind the ninth green on the West Course.

The two waitresses assigned to the table slowly made their way around, collecting the individual orders for drinks and lunch. They worked as fast as they could, but there was always someone on the other side of the table clamoring for a drink or a condiment or something. They did the best they could.

"Hey, I was thinking about the drone project last night on the way home. How would you get the liquid into aerosol form so that it would disperse in a wide enough area to expand the kill zone?" Mike asked.

With this, the waitress nearly dropped the tray of water glasses she was carrying to the table. Sam had noticed her face as she tried to eavesdrop on the conversation.

"They're harmless, not really terrorists. We are merely playing a 'what-if' game about how a group might go about

41

stealing a drone and using it in a terrorist act. You don't have to call the police on them." Sam smiled a polite, reassuring smile.

"Crazy old men," the waitress muttered to her colleague as she passed her going into the kitchen.

"What's up? Those old farts didn't put their hands all over you?"

"No, nothing like that. They're just crazy." Tami loaded her tray with sandwiches that were ready to be brought to the table as she continued. "They are out there bragging about how they can steal a drone and use it to kill people. Please."

"That's too funny. Those guys can't even stand up straight. They are older than my grandpa. The one guy is in a walker for God's sake."

"I know." Tami shook her head. "This is definitely going on Twitter."

CHAPTER 9

JUST OVERHEARD GROUP PLOTTING to steal a drone–CUBI #crazyoldmen. Tami sent the tweet out that afternoon after she had completed her shift. She couldn't believe what she heard and couldn't wait to share it with the world.

When the tweet came across the desk in Brussels, there was laughter on the floor. One tech passed it to another, then another. Soon it was circulating through the entire room, sending a wave of chuckling that rippled from one end of the room to the other.

That all stopped when Vasili walked in. Heads lowered closer to the screens; hands rapidly keying in the next code.

"I want to see what was so funny. Show it to me."

The tech nearest Vasili pulled up the message, then leaned back in his chair so that Vasili could read the screen.

"Who sent this?"

A few keystrokes and the name that belonged to the twitter handle appeared on the screen.

"Where does this person live?"

A flurry of keystrokes, then an address in New Hudson, Michigan, USA appeared.

"Erase that at once."

The screen went blank and Vasili walked out of the room. The tech looked at those next to him. They knew what would come next. Even though they didn't understand why the man in the dark-colored clothing fixated on the seemingly harmless note, it must have meant something they couldn't decipher.

* * *

Arriving at the airport, Vasili caught the first plane headed for Detroit. He arrived before six in the evening and hired a car. His first stop was the address that had appeared on the screen several hours earlier. Now the waiting game began as he parked down the block. Vasili used the scope from his rifle as a spyglass to magnify the details.

The photo from Facebook was etched into his memory as he waited patiently for someone to appear at the house. The neighborhood was quiet that evening. A few neighbors were out walking their dogs, one or two joggers passed by. No one took notice of the man behind the wheel of the parked car.

Around ten o'clock an old, red Ford Tempo parked in front of the house and a young girl matching Tami's description got out, walked up to the door, put her key in the lock, and went inside. He had his first target.

The rest of the night Vasili studied the layout, the others who came and went, everything he would need to know. Promptly at six forty-five the next morning, Tami came out dressed in her waitress uniform. Vasili followed her to work, then sat in his car in the parking lot for an hour until several golfers showed up.

He followed them into the clubhouse, then sat at a table pretending to read the paper he had picked up at the front door.

"Can I bring you some coffee to start?" Tami asked, interrupting his reading.

Vasili didn't acknowledge her presence, but turned over the coffee cup in front of him and waited for it to be filled.

"Cream or sugar?" the young waitress asked.

"No. I'd like two eggs over easy, ham, whole wheat toast, and grape jelly."

"Any juice?"

"No." Vasili never looked up from his paper.

Ten minutes later, his order arrived.

"Can you believe this?" Vasili said with no trace of accent.

"What?"

"It says here that they ordered a drone strike in the Middle East. Some suspected terrorist group was targeted. The missile hit a weapons stockpile somewhere in Syria." Vasili read from the paper.

"Those things scare me. Just the other day, I overheard some men discussing plans to steal one. That's what I can't believe." The cute young waitress put down the plate of food in front of Vasili.

"You don't say?" Vasili's eyebrows widened in mock surprise.

"Who were they? Arabs?"

"No. They were normal. I think they were having some kind of golf outing. There were a lot of them, crazy old men I called them. But they were good tippers. I think one was a member or something..."

"So, you know this guy?"

"Not really. I think his name was Glen, or Greg, or something. He comes in a couple of times a week."

Vasili nodded, then went back to his paper and breakfast. That was the breadcrumb that might prove useful.

After breakfast, he went to the Pro Shop to inquire about an outing. The Pro was an agreeable chap and told him they did that sort of thing all the time.

"Why, only last week we had a group that had their forty-fifth high school reunion here. They golfed in the morning, then had lunch and sat around for quite a while reminiscing. We can accommodate any size group given enough lead time." The Pro gave his best sales pitch about the course, the food, and the other amenities they offered.

After a few more tailored questions, Vasili knew all he needed for now.

He drove to a Sheraton several miles away. Far enough that he wouldn't likely bump into anyone from that morning.

Now he needed to do some research on the group. He googled the school and the reunion and found the website the members used to communicate with each other. Everything he needed was there—names, photos, everything. Now he needed to study the names to select those that might be useful. Two names in particular caught his attention. Perhaps he could piggyback his own black-op after all.

CHAPTER 10

HELEN WAS HAVING TROUBLE ADJUSTING to her newfound freedom. She had spent her entire life working in some fashion. First there was grade school and high school, then nursing school, then her career. She never really had any time that she could call her own, not on any consistent basis, anyway. She didn't know quite what to do with herself after she retired.

Everyone who has ever worked for a living has said they wouldn't have that problem; they would know exactly what to do. Helen was that way too when she was working. She had made so many mental notes of what she wanted to do in retirement.

The problem was, now that it was no longer a dream, the starkness of the reality was crushing. There were too many other considerations. Her aging parents added a sense of guilt that prevented her from planning any round the world cruise. She wouldn't feel comfortable being away for that long. Then there was always the cost. Now that there was no steady paycheck coming in, only a meager pension, and Sam's contract work that was hit and miss, they would have to economize a bit more than they were used to. True, some expenses, such as commuting and lunches in the cafeteria, would no longer be necessary, but that didn't come close to making up the difference between her paycheck and her pension. And those damn politicians were always dipping into her checkbook with the latest wealth transfer legislation. She never considered herself or Sam wealthy until the politicians started in on the calls for higher taxes on the rich. What they meant was people like her who had worked hard all their lives.

Helen quietly went about her life. Even before she retired, she had given some thought to volunteer work and looked into several opportunities. The first was with the church garden club, because she always loved digging in the dirt, even as a child. It made her somehow feel more alive each spring when she watched the flowers she had planted pop their heads through the snow. She wanted to bring this same joy to her fellow parishioners.

It didn't take her long to get into the swing of things. The group was small but friendly. They were more than eager to have another set of hands to help with all the chores that a garden entails. Plus, it got her out of the house once a week and gave her someone different to talk with, someone who shared her love of flowers and digging in the dirt.

Sam, on the other hand, always tethered himself to his computer. His freelance work kept him hopping from time to time. The money was sufficient. Given his skill set, he could have charged his clients more, but he never was good at the business end of things and besides, this way he could pick the assignments that suited his interests and skill set. He was adept at multitasking and could think outside the box in ways that surprised and delighted his clients, always delivering more than he promised. He found joy in finding creative solutions to problems posed to him by his clients.

When Helen got too antsy, he would push away from the computer and take her for a walk downtown. They would window shop and sometimes stop for lunch or dinner. There were plenty of kitschy restaurants to suit any palate.

As Sam and Helen strolled past the fabric store, the conversation drifted back to the reunion.

"Helen? Did I mention the committee is thinking about a destination event for our fiftieth reunion?"

"No, not that I recall."

"Is that something you would be interested in attending?"

"Sure. I love to travel, you know that. I would go anywhere. Not that I know any of the wives or that many of the guys, but as long as there were joint events and things to do while you guys relived your high school memories, that would be okay with me."

"By then, I'm not sure how much we will remember of high school. We will be lucky if we remember to put our socks on."

"Any idea where they might go?"

"They were tossing around Bermuda or another Caribbean Island. It's all tentative. There is a bit of concern that some guys that regularly attend may not be able to afford a destination affair. The whole thing is still up in the air."

"Well, we can plan something on our own. We don't have to wait five more years." Helen offered in an optimistic, almost pleading tone.

"You're funny."

"No, I'm serious. There are things on my bucket list I want to see, Paris in the spring, Japan at Cherry Blossom time, maybe a trip through the Loire Valley. We could stay in Chateaus. I have been reading about all these wonderful old places that have been converted into small and sometimes not so small hotels. It would be perfect. We could visit all the wine caves and tour the countryside." The enthusiasm in Helen's voice reflected her desire for travel.

49

"Sounds expensive."

"It's not too bad. I've checked a bit and as long as we are careful, we should be able to manage one overseas vacation every couple of years."

"Every couple of years?" The trepidation level in Sam's voice rose.

"Sure. We can't see it all at once. We need to take our time to soak in the atmosphere. This is really something that I would like to do, Sam."

"I know. I promise to give it some thought."

The couple walked hand in hand down to the far end of the central business district in silence, then crossed the street to walk back home on the other side. Sam's thoughts centered on how many more jobs he would have to accept in order to get the funds he thought he would need for this additional expense. It was not something he factored into his initial retirement calculations.

CHAPTER 11

"HUH!" VASILI SHOT STRAIGHT UP in a cold sweat, grabbing the crumpled sheets tight in his clenched fists as if startled from some distant reality. The dream of those events, long since banished from his consciousness, had once again arisen. All too familiar were the memories.

The dream that startled Vasili always began the same, with someone bursting through the door, his parents sitting on the couch, two glasses of vodka on a nearby table. It was dark in the apartment with only a single lamp outlining his parents. Vasili had been put to bed hours earlier, but woke up at the sound of something unfamiliar. He rubbed the sleep from his eyes, trying to see his parents. He was walking towards them, wanting to get them to calm him from the nightmare that woke him. All he could see was the flash from the muzzle. Two shots, one aimed at his father, the other at his mother. He screamed in horror, the silent scream that never escapes the lips. He ran to protect his family; the steps stuck in mud that never seem to go anywhere. He watched as the man checked for signs of life, then looked around as he finished the vodka left in the glasses. He raced to the bathroom and hid in the cabinet under the sink as he listened for the man searching the house, looking for him.

It was a panic that filled his soul. He struggled with his breathing, hoping against hope that the hurriedness of his breath would not give him away. Then, after an eternity, a sigh of relief escaped his lips when he heard the footsteps leaving the apartment and of the door slamming shut. Sleep would come in that small cabinet.

In the morning, he dared to come out, hoping that it had all been a nightmare, just as his life would be from that moment forward. The memory would haunt him forever. He looked with disbelief at the single hole in his father's forehead and then at the one in his mother's. How could such a small wound cause so much destruction in his life?

He nudged them, called to them, and pushed them on the shoulder to wake them. Nothing worked. Their skin felt cold to the touch, a blue coloration was visible on their lips and face. He brought them breakfast and ate his while seated on the floor next to the table where the two empty glasses sat. His parents never touched their breakfast.

When it was time for lunch, it was the same. He tried to coax them to eat, repeating the words they often used when he stubbornly refused to eat. It didn't seem to work.

When the soldiers came to take away the bodies of his parents, Vasili hid in the cabinet where he hid the night of the shooting. He slept in the cabinet for the next weeks until there was no more food in the apartment. The finality of his solitude was sinking in. He had no one in the entire world.

Vasili began foraging for food, stealing from an open door, a vendor who wasn't watching, even eating the garbage no one wanted. In the months that followed, several times the soldiers came looking for him, but they never found him. He didn't want to be found. Eventually, the soldiers stopped coming. He was grateful for that. Little did he know that this would only signal the beginning of his struggles. The landlord eventually rented the apartment where he slept out of the cold to strangers. Before they came, he gathered the belongings he could carry and took the gun his parents had hidden in the cushions of the couch, the gun they could not reach when they needed it the most. How he hated that gun, but somehow in the back of his mind he knew he would need it.

The dream had been a haunting memory that remained with him of what was. The days turned into months, the months into years. He wandered the streets, seeking what he could not find.

Ever since Dmitri had found him in Sofia and had taken him under his wing, the dream had vanished. No longer did it fill his every dream. There were a series of foster homes, sometimes in countries that spoke the same language. As he grew older, the foster homes they sent him to were in foreign lands. He spent time in an American high school, learning the language and the customs. He spent his college years in England learning what they offered. After that it was Germany and other countries, other jobs, other training. Dmitri had a purpose to where he sent the lad, always a long-term plan. Most of the time, Vasili was unaware of the purpose. For years at a time, he would not see Dmitri. Then the man would again appear in his life with some special instructions.

Vasili could only think that the memories had resurfaced now because he was back in America and that an American had killed his parents. He hated all Americans. His first assignment was to kill the man who killed his family. Somehow, it was not enough. He needed to kill all of them, punish them for what they had stolen from him. His parents were good, honest, hardworking people, not deserving of the death forced upon them, upon him.

Dmitri never told him that his parents were agents in the employ of the State. He never saw the need to confide in the boy, or the man he became, that his parents were ruthless assassins. He never told him how many Westerners his parents had killed under orders from the State, from Dmitri himself. It was best this way. At least, that is what Dmitri told himself.

Vasili sat up in bed and shook the sleep from his head, the dream from his memory. Slowly he got up, walked to the bathroom and splashed cold water on his face, wiping it with the towel that hung next to the sink. He stared at the glass in front of him, searching for that innocent boy before the nightmare began.

CHAPTER 12

JAMIE WAS WORKING ON A CREATIVE new ad for the Pure Michigan campaign. Her client had a well-established format he wanted followed and a brand with its own DNA. The challenge was coming up with a novel approach that dovetailed with the contract specifications. The previous ads had set the bar high. Now the client needed to build on that foundation and take the campaign to the next level.

Jamie had spent her entire life living in Michigan, and she loved every bit. Rarely had she ever ventured out of the state. Now her task included marketing the state as a vacation destination for people across the country.

Not that there was any shortage of ideas. The problem with her latest project was that there were too many ideas, too many destinations, each tied to a specific childhood memory. She couldn't use all the memories in the campaign, but family friendly memories were certainly a large part of the campaign's DNA.

Though the pressures of the deadlines were mounting, this was a labor of love. More and more she was working late, taking quick lunches, and ordering carryout in order to get a few extra hours of work at the office. She was burning the candle at both ends.

She spent the night preparing for the lunch meeting she had with the client. She would present the preliminary storyboards that pitched three new ideas. There was still way too much work to finish before the meeting. There were so many things she needed to refine and perfect. Never satisfied with her own work, Jamie was the type that saw the flaws in the leaf and rarely saw the perfection of the forest.

Pat understood the late nights and the quest for perfection. He used the free time to practice his guitar and sing his favorite Irish melodies. After a while, he had brought his own work home in order to fill the empty time. His research was under no particular time line. There were no specific checkpoints or deadlines to worry about. He wasn't even the only researcher working on the problem. Researchers around the world, in industry and academia, were doing similar work. It gave him a sense of oneness with his colleagues.

Often Pat longed to travel to some conference in order to share ideas and opinions with like-minded scientists. How he yearned for the constructive debate that refined the raw ore of ideas into the artfully crafted metal of invention. He loved ecology and the environment. For as long as he could remember, he had been a tree hugger. He wore the badge proudly. He wanted to save the world, or at least make it a better place. It was something he thought about often.

Even in the mundane aspects of life, he was always trying to simplify, to reduce, reuse, and recycle. He developed a folded sequence, sort of origami for packaging, that would allow a user to reseal any open plastic or foil bag without a chip clip. He was always thinking about saving the world from environmental pollution.

His work required an extensive amount of experimentation with accelerated growing techniques. Not only did the algae have to have the right chemical structure; it had to grow quickly and with little energy input. He needed to find a way to grow the algae in closed compartments, like tubes, so that someone could eventually process large batches in a manner not unlike a chemical refinery. There were billions of gallons of gasoline consumed every day, so any fuel that had any hope of taking its place needed to be produced at an extremely fast rate in order to benefit from the economy of scale.

Pat had built a makeshift refinery of sorts in his backyard. It allowed him to test various techniques for growth acceleration. He had even published a couple of papers on his findings. They were nothing spectacular or worthy of a Nobel Prize or anything, but they helped advance the science. He was very proud of his contribution, though the neighbors didn't always share his fascination with that contraption in the backyard.

CHAPTER 13

MEHANATA'S ON THE LOWER EAST SIDE of New York on Ludlow Street, was where Vasili knew he would find what he needed most. The food was tolerable, and the ice cage in the back offered the finest selection of vodka in the country.

When he arrived that day, the familiar sounds of Bulgarian music blasted through the sound system. A Gypsy belly dancer entertained the crowd as the patrons sat on porch swings. Posters and signs of all kinds decorated the walls in an eclectic pattern reminiscent of the torn down and papered over signs typical of any college campus.

Vasili pushed his way through the crowd to the lower level, where a DJ played music as an even larger crowd jammed shoulder to shoulder, tried to move in time to the music. The smell of sweat from hung heavy in the air. It was a wild group unconstrained by the conventions of polite society.

Vasili made his way through the dance floor to where the door to the ethereal ice cage stood. The bouncer took one look at him and waved him in. There would be no cover charge for this patron. Nor did Vasili don one of the Soviet military uniforms offered. It wouldn't be necessary in those Siberian conditions. Once inside, the subtle bread-like aroma of Russian Standard Vodka filled the room. Lining the back wall was every type of vodka imaginable. Beluga, Stolichnaya, Stolichnaya Gold, Moskovskaya, Pshenichnaya, Dovgan, Kubanskaya, Rodnik, Strelestkaya, Pertsovka, Limonnaya, Gzlzelka, Matryoshkina, Zarskava, Navigator, Pskovskaya, Yat, Slavyankaya, and Staraya Sloboda. The bartender handed him a shot glass made from ice. Vasili nodded to the Standard, and the bartender filled the glass. Vasili downed the glass and slammed it back on the bar. Five more times, this simple gesture was repeated. When Dmitri finished the sixth shot, the bartender nodded to the man at the door, who escorted Vasili to the back room.

Natasha was at her usual table. Her jet-black hair, cropped short, gave a playfully deceptive appearance. Her long slender right leg, wrapped in black silk stockings, extended beyond the edge of the table, visible to anyone who might glance in that direction. When she saw Vasili approach, she didn't rise to greet him or offer her hand. She knew what he wanted and why he came. She simply nodded for him to take a seat and the man who had accompanied Vasili to the back room returned to his post.

"I need not ask why you are here or who you are." Natasha said, eying the man across from her.

"I need your services." Vasili offered. He placed his Makarov on the table between them.

"How many and when?"

"Two will do and they can come in two weeks." He pulled a slip of paper from his pocket and pushed it across the table to the woman seated opposite him.

"Very well." Natasha was not one to require details. In her line of work, it was best not to know anything. She was the broker.

Vasili pulled an envelope from his pocket and placed it on the table. It was sufficiently thick that Natasha nodded and swept it up, placing it on her lap out of view below the edge of the table. "Will there be anything else?"

Vasili picked up the Makarov and put it in the holster behind his back. He walked out of the room, returning to the noise of the discotheque. Before exiting, he made his way to the restroom along the side wall. The gray marble tile that covered the walls and floor contrasted with the oak on the doors and stainless-steel dividers. The bold red color of the urinals made them stand out as a visible image. Their unique shape resembled an open mouth complete with teeth, suggesting a playful tone. The sink was equally suggestive. A stainless-steel basin balanced precariously on the back of a naked woman's slender form, bent over at the waist. The bright red legs spread slightly apart. One had to approach the red porcelain bottom closely in order to gain access to the water taps. Above the sink was a mirror and a sign asking the patrons to be kind to Lilly.

The thought that the sink had a name was amusing to Vasili. Somehow, it reminded him of his days living on the streets.

CHAPTER 14

VASILI RETURNED TO DETROIT and continued his research. He studied the profiles of the classmates and learned all he could about them. Eventually, he selected the two most likely to be of use to him. It was then that he began his own surveillance.

Outside the Northville residence, he studied the comings and goings of the two occupants. Sometimes the occupants left together. Often, they left at different times. There was some randomness to their movements, but sufficient commonality that he could deal with.

When the house was empty, he entered through the back door, his hands carefully covered in black leather driving gloves. He quickly tapped into the computer and convinced himself that there was a sufficient level of talent suited to his needs. Skillfully, he went about installing a camera carefully hidden between some books on the mantle. Vasili installed another camera in the den to monitor the work routine. When the link was established to his smartphone, he looked around the room to ensure everything was as it was when he had entered. Convinced the set up was sufficient, he exited the way he came in.

The surveillance time in Northville alternated with that of the home in Pontiac. There, he was more at ease with the tree cover that guarded the street. It was more to his liking, the darkness, and the location away from any streetlight. As he had done in the other residence, Vasili set up a similar monitoring system.

His next task was to pick up several used computers. He placed an ad in the Arab American Times offering a bit more than the typical going rate for previously owned laptops and tablets. The ad specified the processor and capabilities. It didn't take long for responses to come in. Vasili contacted several individuals in the Dearborn area and made the cash purchases. Each time, he was wearing a unique set of clothing and a different facial disguise. He purchased far more equipment than he estimated he would need.

He examined each computer thoroughly in his hotel room. He selected the most promising ones and stacked them up in the order he wanted them to be used, charging each laptop.

* * *

Surveillance of the two homes continued for some time. Each day, he studied the comings and goings of one of the key individuals. On Monday it was Sam, Tuesday it was Pat, Wednesday it was Jamie, and Thursday it was Helen.

Helen's day began with early morning mass. Vasili waited outside while the service was underway. He walked around the building and the yard, studying it from every angle. Nowhere did he write anything down. He never forgot a detail.

After church, Vasili followed Helen to the Kroger store. He went inside and bought a few items as he walked up and down the aisles. When Helen went to the fabric store, he did not follow her. Instead, he elected to wait in the parking lot. After the errands, Helen returned home. The pattern of her daily routine seemed random, except for morning mass.

Jamie's routine was more predictable. She went to work at the same time each morning and then, around noon, she left the building and walked to a cafe in downtown Birmingham for lunch. Most days it was a quick lunch, then back to the office. Quite often, her office was the last light to go off in the building. Vasili admired the dedication to detail that she must exhibit. It was one of her best qualities. It was always a pleasure to follow her around town. She appeared to have a pleasant disposition and was friendly with those she met on the street, always did with a kind word for those who greeted her. Vasili paid close attention to the clothes she wore, professional yet not dull, bold but not flamboyant, stylish but not noticeably so. It was an appealing mix of fabric and color, quite in contrast with the dingy black he wore. His clothing was calculated to fade into the background.

Pat, on the other hand, had a varied work schedule. Some days he was in the office, other days he was working in the field. The field locations were all over Southeastern Michigan. It was very difficult to predict where he would be at any hour of the day—that is until it came time for dinner. Each day at exactly five-thirty, he would pull into his driveway and walk into the house. That part of the routine was predictable.

Sam was the homebody of Vasili's little study group. He rarely left the house except in the evenings for his walk. He would be an easy target to pick off when the time came.

Over the next two weeks, Vasili studied the individuals, varying which day he monitored which person. None of them posed any threat to him. It was just that he needed their 'cooperation' without the interference of nosy neighbors. He would need at least a day head start with no interference to get things moving in a positive direction.

Vasili had located a vacant warehouse on Schaeffer in Dearborn. The location was quiet, but not isolated, near Metro airport and close to the Ambassador Bridge that could get them quickly into Canada. He had several options at his disposal in the event things went sideways. There was always a plan B and a plan C.

When his two temporary accomplices arrived, he met them two blocks from the warehouse and briefed them on their assignments. They went through a series of dry runs between the various locations they would likely visit. Vasili laid out a rigid time line and provided a set of photographs of the targets and the locations. These were to be destroyed after the group memorized them.

The first thing in the morning, two vehicles were procured. The men took the license plates off the stolen vehicles and switched them with two other vehicles.

CHAPTER 15

HELEN LINGERED AFTER MASS at Our Lady of Victory. As a member of the altar society, it was her turn to collect the soiled altar linens and bring them home to be washed. The linens, especially the ones that were used to wipe the chalice, needed to be cared for separately. The water used to wash them couldn't be sent through the pipes into the sewer. That was unacceptable and a sacrilege. The used water needed to be deposited directly into the ground, where it could bring life to the grass and plants.

There was a special sink in the sacristy for this purpose that led to an outside dry well. Sometimes the ladies washed the linens in that sink. Today, Helen collected the linens in a clear Rubbermaid container and carried them to her car. She would launder them at home, properly disposing of the water in her garden, then carefully iron and fold the cloths to be returned the following day, neatly pressed in that same container.

Helen was alone when she walked from the church to her car, the box of altar linens snuggled safely in her arms, the strap of her purse over her shoulder and the bag nestled tightly under her arm. She never noticed the car parked next to hers, pressed in so tightly that she wouldn't be able to get into the driver's side door. As she approached her car on the passenger side, an ominous sense of impending danger came over her.

In an instant, two men grabbed her. One man covered her mouth. The other man grabbed her legs and pushed her into the back seat of the white Chevy Cavalier. He followed her into the vehicle, holding her down, pressing her to the floor. The box of linens was left on the asphalt.

The driver calmly walked around the car, got in, and drove off. With one hand, the assailant in the back seat opened Helen's purse and took out her phone, switching it off. No one would disturb them.

By the time the two assailants had arrived at their destination, Helen was bound and gagged. The garage door was closed before anyone exited the car. The man in the back had injected a needle into her arm. Her body was limp on the floor of the car.

When the men entered the house, Vasili had already gagged Sam and tied him to a chair in the kitchen. Sam's eyes widened as he watched the two strangers enter the house from the garage. He was expecting Helen to come to his rescue. One man injected him with a needle and Sam's body slumped forward in the chair. The other man brought in Helen's purse and laid it on the kitchen counter. It wasn't long before Sam was lying on the back seat of the white Chevy Cavalier, once again reunited with his wife.

The assailant went back into the home and plugged a timer into one light in the living room. It would appear to the outside world that the Kennedys had gone on a brief vacation.

* * *

Jamie had just finished her lunch meeting at Mitchell's in Birmingham. She was walking back to the ad agency where she could finally get to work assembling the approved storyboards into a finished product. It had been a very satisfying meeting. The client loved two of the concepts and, with a few simple modifications, they would also approve the third.

It was a mistake to cut through the parking lot, after the lunch crowd and before the dinner crowd, but she was in a hurry. She was never one to take long lunches, but the client insisted on micromanaging the project and ordered several minor changes. Jamie's voice was upbeat as she was talking into an app that allowed her to record her thoughts from the meeting, the changes the client suggested. She quickly passed between the rows of cars parked behind the businesses that fronted Woodward.

The man appeared from nowhere and grabbed the slender woman from behind. He covered her mouth with a rag soaked in chloroform. His partner approached with the car and soon Jamie's body was deposited in the back seat. Her phone had dropped from her hand, still recording the sound of the tires as they moved farther away.

The vehicle turned out of the parking lot and headed north toward Pontiac.

When the car arrived outside her home, the driver made his way inside and collected the remaining occupant. Pat was already drugged and lying on the floor.

"Why did he drug him? What if someone sees us carrying the body?"

"Quiet, you fool. He knows what he is doing."

* * *

It was nightfall when the second couple was brought to the warehouse near the Dearborn city hall. They abandoned the cars used in the kidnapping on the streets far from the warehouse;

the keys left in the ignition. The vehicles would not last long in their current locations.

Vasili arrived in a van he had procured that morning. He handed the keys to the two men standing over the four limp bodies. "The women are yours. They are not to be harmed until I give the order."

There was no need for the men to argue or even acknowledge the command. They knew better. They loaded the women into the van and pulled out of the warehouse for the long journey.

Vasili looked at the two men lying in on the concrete floor in front of him.

Pathetic, he thought. How could two grown men allow themselves to be so easily captured? Now he would need to convince them he meant business, that they had no choice but to cooperate.

CHAPTER 16

WHEN THE USUAL CROWD of faithful worshipers arrived for morning mass at Our Lady of Victory, the first to enter the parking lot couldn't help but notice white Cavalier. It wasn't unusual for some to arrive early. What seemed out of place was the plastic container with the altar linens strewn about in the parking lot. No parishioner would be so careless as to drop the linens on the ground, let alone leave them and walk away.

Inside the narthex, those gathering chatted among themselves, trying to determine whose car that was and why the cloths were on the ground. Lisa and Gertrude took it upon themselves to pick up the linens and bring them back into the Church. They hadn't been cleaned, so one of them would have to take them home after Mass.

It wasn't until Mary arrived that they learned Helen had been the one responsible for washing the linens that week. No one could remember if she had actually picked them up or whether someone had broken into the Church and was rummaging around vandalizing the Sacristy.

The women search the sacristy and nothing seemed to be missing, not the gold chalices, nor any of the vestments, and the Poor Box was intact. It didn't appear to be a robbery.

When Helen didn't show up for Mass, the ladies began to worry. Helen hadn't missed Mass since she retired. No one could recall any mention of Helen leaving town or having some early morning doctor's appointment, so Mary took it upon herself to call Helen. There was no answer.

"I'm pretty sure that's Helen's car over there where you found the linens." Bernie remarked. "This doesn't look right. I think something's wrong."

Bernie was the self-appointed acolyte of the church. Long ago, Father had given him a key, as he was always the first to arrive for daily mass. He would light the altar candles, put out the lectionary, and open the book to the correct readings for morning mass. He would turn on the lights in the winter and heating system when he was cold. In his concern for his fellow parishioner, he dialed nine-one-one and reported the incident, vague as the details might be.

The Northville police arrived a few minutes later in front of the church. The two officers examined the car and walked around the area. They spoke to those who were part of the usual weekday mass crowd. All they learned was that nothing seemed out of place but the car and the linens. Nothing else was missing from the Church.

Bernie had informed the officers of the name of the owner of the white car that seemed to be abandoned in the parking lot.

When the police arrived at the Kennedy's home, they knocked on the front door and no one answered. The two officers walked around the house and checked the backyard, then the rear door. It was unlocked.

"Police, is anyone home." The officer announced as he walked into the door, one hand on his service revolver. There was no answer. The department had little experience with missing persons. Those kinds of things happened in big cities, not small, close-knit communities.

The officers phoned in the information then began going door to door to see if any of the neighbors could provide any information. Had anyone seen the people who lived in the house? When was the last time they spoke to them?

A few people had seen a car the night before, a dark sedan, but no one knew who it belonged to or had bothered to collect the license number.

The circle of those who knew about the incident was expanding geometrically. Neighbors were calling neighbors, close friends began calling the Kennedy family members trying to locate Helen and Sam as it was unusual for him not to be home. He was always home. After all, he worked from home on most days.

The ever-expanding circle brought the officers no closer to finding any useful information. The best they could determine was that the white Chevy Cavalier in the church parking lot did, in fact, belong to Helen. But why was it there and how long had it been there?

* * *

When Jamie didn't come back from lunch, it was no genuine cause for concern. The office had an open policy and people came and went to meetings on their own schedule. It wasn't unusual for someone to be in before sun up or stay long after the sun went down.

What was unusual was the fact that Jamie wasn't there by noon the following day. The office manager took notice and began asking around. Her work space didn't seem to be touched and there were no meetings on her calendar. It wasn't like Jamie not to show up. When she worked from home, typically she called in.

So, by the end of the day when no one had heard from Jamie, the manager began calling, first the cell number, then the home number, and finally the number of her emergency contact, Pat. Even though there was no answer at any of the numbers, the manager didn't think it was her place to notify authorities. That was the responsibility of her emergency contact.

It was Pat's younger brother, Chris, who finally called police two days later. He had received a call from their mother, who had been trying to get in touch with Pat about some financial papers she had received in the mail. Pat was always the one to explain the documents to her and tell her what she was supposed to do with them. Not that she was old; she was only eighty-eight, but she needed the confidence of checking these things with her oldest son ever since her husband had passed away seven years ago. When Pat hadn't called her back, she had called Chris and asked him to call his brother.

When the Pontiac police arrived to investigate, they found the back door to the home open. Inside, there was no one. The officers posted a missing person's alert went back to patrolling the area. Missing persons were common in Pontiac and the police didn't take them too seriously until after a week had passed.

CHAPTER 17

IN THE MIDDLE OF THE WAREHOUSE was a single, dirty folding table. Pushed against the table was a single chair. A laptop sat in the center of the table. Next to the laptop was a photograph of two women. They appeared to be sleeping. When he awoke, Sam found his body taped to the chair. He was alone. He stared at the photograph, then at the laptop, then back at the photo.

As the haze lifted from the chemical injection, he recognized one of the sleeping women. He struggled to free himself from the tape.

Moments later, Vasili walked up behind him. "Good evening."

Startled to find he wasn't alone, Sam turned to see who was speaking.

"Don't try to get away. You have no doubt realized that I also have your wife. To answer the question you are now formulating, yes, she is still alive, as is Jamie Mobley."

The look on Sam's face told him the name meant little to him.

"Perhaps I should have said Pat O'Connor's significant other. And yes, I also have Pat. He is in the office over there." Vasili pointed to the back of the empty room.

"If you do exactly what you are told, no harm will come to the women. You have my word. I am not the type to kill innocent civilians."

Sam looked into Vasili's eyes. Somehow, he didn't believe the man. "Why have you kidnapped me? Us?"

"Not kidnapped, borrowed. I have need of your special talents." Vasili's voice was calm, unemotional.

"I have nothing you need." Sam was agitated and worried.

"Don't be so modest. You have a unique skill set that few can duplicate."

A puzzled look filled Sam's face.

"You have a gift with computers. I've been studying the complexity of some of the software applications you've written. They are exquisite in their theory, power, and grace. You can take the complex and make it simple enough that an imbecile could use even the most advanced technology."

Sam still didn't comprehend his role in all this.

"See that laptop? I want you to write an application that could control a drone."

"Impossible." Sam's lips tightened as a stern look overtook his face.

"Not impossible. Difficult perhaps, but not impossible. I have been advised that the easiest point of entry is to hack into NASA and procure the ground command software package. Then I want you to modify the software to suit my needs."

Sam shook his head. "I won't help you." He crossed his arms in front of his chest and sat back in the chair.

"Suit yourself." Vasili tapped the photo on the table.

Sam's arms fell as he lowered his head in resignation.

"Don't hurt them."

"I've already given my word. The rest is entirely up to you."

His body still taped to the chair, Sam inched closer to the table by the awkward movement of his feet pulling his body and the chair. "Do we even have a signal in here?"

"There is a Wi-Fi hotspot in the Hookah lounge next door." Vasili pointed his finger in the signal's direction.

Sam turned on the laptop and checked the signal's strength. It would be sufficient. Sam typed quickly and efficiently, first searching Wikipedia to learn what he could about drones and how they operated. Link after link, he followed until he felt he knew enough to begin. With a flurry of keystrokes, Sam gained access to target mainframe and located the likely files he would need. The download began.

"Mind if I untape myself?" Sam was growing restless from being confined to the chair.

Vasili moved next to Sam and cut through the tape that was holding him in position. Sam stood up and stretched his legs as he removed the pieces of tape stuck to his body. The stiffness in his limbs told him he had been in that position for quite a while. For the first time, Sam noticed the mustiness of his surroundings. He couldn't tell where he was, but he could hear the occasional car on the streets outside.

When the download was complete, Sam disconnected from the internet and started the program. It opened correctly. He seemed to have all the pieces he would require.

"I want you to transfer the files to this computer." Vasili handed Sam a different laptop.

"Why?"

Vasili didn't answer.

When the file transfer was complete and Vasili was convinced the program worked, he turned off the first computer and took it from the room. He walked out the back door, wiped the computer down, and dumped the computer in the industrial waste bin behind the lounge.

"Well, the program seems to work. Now what?"

"We need to change the command structure so that the 'on the loop' operator doesn't notice a problem once we gain control of the drone. We don't want him reestablishing a link or issuing a self-destruct command." Vasili seemed to have thought this project through.

"That will take some time."

Vasili nodded, tapping his finger once again on the photo.

By noon the next day, Sam had completed the initial modifications he felt would be necessary. An empty wrapper from the egg McMuffin was on the floor under the table keeping the three empty coffee cups company.

"I need some sleep." Sam rubbed his face with his hands. The adrenaline mixed with coffee was no longer sufficient.

Vasili nodded and pointed to the office.

In the corner of the room was a cot. Pat was sitting in the chair behind the desk.

"You okay, Pat?" Sam asked as he walked into the office.

"Sam? What are you doing here?" Surprised to see a friendly face. He feared he was alone in this predicament. Not that he understood why he was being held.

"Same as you. They have Jamie and Helen." Sam's voice conveyed his concern for the two women.

"What? Where are they?" Pat said.

"I don't know. I have only seen a photo of them."

"How many guards are outside?" Pat had formulated several plans for escape in his mind. Now he had a reason to try one of them.

"I've only seen the one—black leather jacket, menacing look."

"That's the only one I've seen. He said if I left the office, he would shoot me."

"I know why I am here, but what does he need with you?" Sam wasn't thinking clearly anymore. He needed to sleep for a few hours.

Pat shrugged his shoulders. "Why does he want you?"

"He wants me to steal a drone."

"What? You're kidding? Why would he want that?"

It was Sam's turn to shrug. "You don't think?"

"What?"

"No, it's not possible."

"You're not thinking they somehow overheard our rambling conversation at the reunion, do you?" Pat began recalling the 'what-if' fantasy they had discussed a few weeks earlier.

"Not possible. We know everyone that was there. I trust every single guy in that room." Sam was confident that none of their classmates had betrayed them.

It was then that a light bulb went off in Sam's consciousness. "But not at the country club. We brought it up again at lunch, remember?"

The new knowledge did little to clarify their current situation.

"I'm sorry Pat. I've been up all night. I need a few hours of sleep."

Pat sat quietly for some time as his friend slept on the cot. Growing restless, Pat went to the door and stuck his head out.

"Can I come out?" he asked, shouting into the vacant warehouse.

"Yes," came the distant reply.

Pat walked out. His first stop was the men's room next door. When he came out, he walked towards the table in the center of the room. The first thing he saw was the photo.

"Are they still alive?"

Vasili nodded.

"Where are they? Can I see them?"

This time, there was no acknowledgement that he asked a question.

"What do you want from me?"

"Your usefulness will be clear after your friend finishes with his part."

By now, Pat knew enough that any follow-up questions were useless.

CHAPTER 18

ATTENDANCE AT THE WEEKDAY MASS at Our Lady of Victory grew steadily in the days following the incident in the parking lot. The church served the needs of a small but close-knit community. It was one of those parishes, not unlike those in a small town, where everyone seemed to know everyone. They cared for each other and looked in on each other when the need arose.

It was not out of the ordinary that Father Clemens, the pastor, took special note of the events in his homily.

"We read in Isaiah that 'God's ways are not our ways.' None of us can understand why anyone would kidnap our beloved Helen or why they would choose to do it from the very parking lot only a few feet away from God's House. Even in this, we must see the hand of God. Know this. God did not harm our friend. He did not do this to her as a punishment or for any other reason. It was out of love for us that He endowed mankind with a free will—the freedom to choose between good and evil, right and wrong. This individual or gang, whoever they are, did evil. They did wrong, ignored the will of God. I am confident they will be found and brought to justice, if not in this world, then in the next. I am confident our Helen will be returned safely to us. I firmly believe that. We pray today for her safe return and for the intentions of all those here present."

After Mass, the congregation lingered in the narthex, hoping to find some new bit of information, the latest development in the case. Mary related again how she knew something was wrong when she discovered the linens strewn about in the parking lot. Someone noted that Sam was also missing and that the police had discovered the house unlocked. This caused a new stir among the crowd gathered that morning. The news that the perpetrators had lingered in the neighborhood was disturbing. How could someone come into their community without being seen by anyone? It made little sense.

Several parishioners had related the conversations they had with the local police about the incident. Some had even been questioned as recently as the day before. All remarked about the frustration expressed by the police that they could not uncover any solid leads, no unusual fingerprints in the house or on the car. Still, the police followed up on even the smallest piece of information, least it later turned out to be important. None of the information led anywhere.

It was the same on the streets of downtown Northville. You couldn't walk the streets or enter a shop without overhearing a conversation related to the kidnapping. Women worried they would be next. Ladies more tightly held onto their purses and made it a point to travel in pairs or in small groups. Mothers scolded their children for straying more than a few feet. No one traveled alone on what was once thought to be the safest streets in America.

CHAPTER 19

PAT'S MOTHER WAS NOW CALLING the Pontiac police every morning at exactly eight o'clock. She had been told frequently that she had to wait for the shift change before she could call, so she waited as long as she could. Every morning the desk Sergeant told her the same thing. There was no new information to report. Still, she wanted him to repeat what they knew. Each morning he patiently repeated the story that he had now memorized, that the police had found the back door unlocked, no fingerprints had been found at the scene, and that both her son and a woman named Jamie Mobley had been reported missing. The fact that nothing was stolen from the house, that their stash of cash was intact in the cabinet in the kitchen to the left of the stove, was important to the police. Just why Mrs. O'Connor couldn't understand.

After she hung up with the police, she would call her son Chris. It was his turn to repeat the story to his mother. Recalling different incidents that he could remember. Occasionally, he would remind her who this Jamie woman was and why the police kept bringing up her name. Somehow, she could never remember that her son was living with a woman. Perhaps she didn't want to remember that part. After all, Mrs. O'Connor was a good Catholic. She had tried to raise her sons to be good

Catholics. While others might look the other way on the new morality, it was not in her to do the same. Not that she had anything against Jamie. They were always pleasant to each other, and Mrs. O'Connor had even asked the woman to help her update the décor in her bedroom. It was the living arrangements that got to her once in a while.

Chris was always patient with his mom's call. He understood her need to talk through these things, trying to keep everything straight in her brain. He often suspected that it was a bit of dementia that was creeping in, causing her to repeat things in specific patterns. The prospect of dealing with an aging parent was unsettling, especially if Pat never showed up again.

Occasionally, Chris would stop by Pat's house to cut the grass or pick up the newspapers and mail that had accumulated. Sometimes the neighbors would stop him and ask if there were any updates. It was always the same. He had nothing to tell them, though sometimes he cursed them in his mind for not paying closer attention the night they kidnapped his brother. He, too, needed to blame someone for what happened.

CHAPTER 20

WHEN HELEN AND JAMIE WOKE, they were sitting in Natasha's office in the lower level of Mehanata's. They found themselves alone in an unfamiliar room in an unfamiliar building.

Helen was the first to wake. Someone had removed the zip ties that bound her hands and the gag from her mouth. This was curious, as she had yet to comprehend where she was or what had happened. "Who are you?"

Startled by the sound of an unfamiliar voice, Jamie rubbed her eyes and sat up. She stared at Helen, not knowing if she was friend or foe. "Why did you bring me here?"

"Bring you? You're not behind this?" Helen was confused. Why was she here with another woman?

"No, they kidnapped me. I'm guessing you were too?" The picture was no clearer for Jamie.

"Yes. But why?" Helen stared at the other woman, trying to determine if she knew her.

Jamie shrugged her shoulders, walked over to the door, and found it locked. She sat back on the couch and looked at Helen. The two women got acquainted, trying to establish some common ground. They learned the details of where they were from. They were not quite neighbors, but they were from the same general area. What they couldn't establish was any connection, any element that would tie them together and explain why they were in a room together, or where they were.

Periodically, someone would unlock the door and bring in a tray of food and water and escort them to the facilities. They were allowed no farther down the hall than the restroom and a woman was with them at all times. Those who came refused to answer even the simplest question.

Above them, they could hear the music in the evenings, but even that provided no discernible clue to their location that they could unravel.

When the guard bringing food commented once that Jamie reminded him of Lilly, not even that provided any context they could understand.

There was but a single couch in the office and the women took turns sleeping on it. The other usually slept on the floor, or simply paced around their prison cell. It was infuriating not knowing the where or why. Besides the couch, there was an ornate wooden desk and a fine wooden chair. The shelves behind the desk were filled with books.

The women had tried asking the guard's questions, but they provided no information beyond some crude comment on their looks. The guards kept their distance from the women, who didn't represent any threat.

"Someone will eventually discover we are missing and call the police." Jamie's comment was more hope than fact.

"Sure. Any day now someone will find us." Helen was trying to be optimistic, but she couldn't understand why Sam hadn't come looking for her or how she could get in touch with him to let him know where she was. They had tried the phone on the desk, but there was no dial tone, no way for them to communicate. She was worrying about Sam and how lonely and worried he must be.

DRONE

Jamie reached over and placed her hand on top of Helen's. Overcome with emotion, Helen began weeping. She leaned over and wrapped her arms around her new best friend. Together they sobbed in each other's arms.

CHAPTER 21

EARLY IN THE MORNING, Vasili had packed up the van with the extra computer gear and the other odds and ends that would be needed, including Pat and Sam. The van pulled out of the warehouse as the early morning dew lifted from the scuffed grass that lined the alley. Traveling south on Schafer towards the interstate, Vasili settled in for the long drive ahead.

Opting to avoid the Ohio Turnpike, the trip to West Virginia would take seven hours down Interstate seventy-five and US twenty-three through Columbus before heading east on US fifty. The last hundred and fifty miles would take the trio through small rural towns in southern Ohio and the northern edge of West Virginia.

Sam recognized the area when they pulled out of the warehouse. It was a part of Dearborn near to where some of his friends from high school grew up. There weren't many kids from the St. Alphonsus area, but he had been over in the area once or twice back then. Some landmarks were familiar, but many of the shops and restaurants had changed hands many times in the past forty-five years.

Pat seemed to recognize the area too. "Is this where you are keeping the women?"

Vasili only shook his head. He was not one to provide details unnecessarily.

"Can you at least tell us if they are in Michigan?" Sam looked up from his computer, thinking he might have better luck communicating with their captor. After all, they had spent the night in close proximity. Surely some connection had been established, however slight.

He got no further than Pat did.

When they turned onto the interstate headed towards Toledo, Sam wondered if they were going to the Space Center to steal the drone. It made a bit of sense. It would probably be easier to steal one from a non-military installation. The security would be less stringent. "So? We're headed to Florida?"

Vasili stared blankly at the road ahead. He was concentrating on staying with traffic but not exceeding the speed limit. Nothing that would attract the attention to any patrol cars that might be in the area. He had warned his two guests that they were not to signal the police, as there would be repercussions down the road. "Lest you're thinking about doing something stupid, like having me arrested on the interstate, I should tell you that if I don't check in every three hours with the boss, he will kill his guests. He has no qualms about civilian casualties like I do."

Of course, Vasili was the one calling all the shots, but it didn't hurt to imply otherwise when it suited his purpose. He still needed the cooperation of his companions.

CHAPTER 22

IT WAS WARM FOR LATE MAY in Michigan when Agents Cooper and Patten arrived to assist the Detroit Field Office. Someone had alerted the Cyber Division after the NASA mainframe had been breached. The trail led to an IP address on the south side of Dearborn.

There were twenty-two mosques within a five-mile radius of the location that the breach had originated from. It would take more resources than the Detroit Field Office had available to put eyes on all of them.

The initial search targeted the area in the immediate vicinity. They enlisted local police to canvas the area. A young boy had commented that he saw two men with beards talking behind the Hookah lounge. The agents made a note of the fact.

Cooper and Patten started their investigation inside the lounge talking with the owner, the staff, anyone who was on site during the time of the breach. They learned that on the night in question; the crowd was typical, a few hundred people who came and went over the course of the evening. Some people stayed only briefly to pick up carryout, some lingered the entire evening. It didn't seem that anyone kept track of anything. Even the receipts were not helpful, as nearly every patron paid in cash. It was the nature of the business and the clientele. But then the agents didn't expect to learn much. The pair sat for a while, monitoring the crowded, smoke-filled room.

They had their laptop connected to the hot-spot allowing them to monitor any other patrons connected to the same signal. There was the usual pattern of activity, some were emailing back and forth to sites in Iraq, Iran, Syria, UAE, others were linked to mosques and Islamic cultural centers downloading foreign language documents, mostly Muslim prayers, others appeared more suspicious as they incited calls to Jihad.

Cooper and Patten attempted to determine which patron was accessing which site. They surreptitiously photographed some individuals and made some notes. Whenever they questioned a patron, it was always the same. No one offered anything helpful and most accused the agents of illegal profiling. There was more than a little hostility in the room.

After a few wasted hours, the pair walked out back and observed three men in the alley smoking and talking in hushed tones. Each man had a beard and was wearing a taqiyah. When they saw the agents, each man immediately snuffed out their smoke and vanished in a different direction. They had left before either agent could snap an image.

Cooper looked up and down the alley for any surveillance cameras, but there were none to be found. Walking back inside, they questioned the staff, but no one seemed to have an opinion who the men might be.

* * *

At the morning briefing at the Dearborn Police Headquarters, Cooper and Patten related the events, and some officers noted the alley had been the location of several arrests, mostly for drugs, but some bookmaking. There was never anything terrorist related they had uncovered. Still, it was something Cooper and Patten thought should be followed up on. Each made a mental note to canvas the alley, looking for additional clues.

It was after lunch when they finally made it back to the location. On a hunch, they took a chance on their least favorite investigative activity, dumpster diving.

"It's your turn Pat. I did it last week outside that sleazy bar in Los Angeles."

"Yeah, that was gross."

Patten donned a set of plastic disposable rain gear and banged on the bin with the butt end of his weapon before climbing in. What he discovered was a putrefying mix of rotting residue from the tobacco remnant of the shisha pipes, Arabic language newspapers, and the decaying remains of food scraped off of plates. The damp liquid from the pipes congealed into a festering concoction that had attracted more than the normal amount of rats, no doubt addicted to the nicotine.

Patten closed his eyes and dipped his gloved hand into the filth, moving it carefully around least he cut himself on some sharp object. The last thing he wanted was to get an open wound in this amalgamation. The bacteria would race like sharks to the scent of fresh blood.

It didn't take long to locate a laptop. It was the only solid item in the dumpster that his hand could detect. Though the computer was damaged, it wasn't destroyed, so there was some hope of recovering something useful. When he opened the lid on the computer, the screen had been cracked and the battery appeared to be dead. Patten handed the machine to Cooper and climbed out of the dumpster. He had enough diving for the afternoon. Patton quickly discarded the now damp rain gear into the dumpster and shuddered as he removed the plastic booties that covered his dingy brown wing tips. The very thought of the putrefying smell that lingered on the discarded clothing was enough to make him puke. The two agents headed back to the Detroit office to examine their find.

* * *

Once back in the office, it didn't take long to verify that they had found the machine used to hack into NASA. They also discovered someone had wiped the computer clean of all fingerprints and DNA evidence and, as expected, they found a partially wiped hard drive. It would take the next several hours to recover the lost fragments of files.

The fully restored drive presented the next challenge. It had to be dissected file by file. The effort was worth the time, as what they learned was most helpful.

CHAPTER 23

"NASA CONFIRMED TODAY that someone had hacked into their mainframe a spokesperson for the Agency said today in a press release. Reportedly no mission sensitive data was taken, and no identities were stolen." Melissa Gilbert from Channel Seven reported on the evening news.

"Thanks Melissa, when we contacted the FBI, they wouldn't talk on the record but told us off the record that they don't yet know the identity of the hacker or hackers. They confirmed the hackers routed their signal through several IP addresses, including locations in China and the Philippines. We don't know what the Chinese might want with the information from NASA. Other Security experts we spoke with told us that Chinese hackers had been testing out the security of various governmental sites, suggesting that a much wider security breach would turn up in the days and weeks ahead. The FBI would not comment further."

The news report never mentioned the Dearborn connection, and the FBI was not about to let out that piece of intelligence. They had enough on their plate dealing with representatives from the Center for Arab-American Relations who were already threatening legal action if the FBI didn't stop profiling individuals of Middle Eastern descent. The Detroit field office was used to being behind the eight ball when it came to neighborhood relations. If it wasn't one ethnic group complaining about poor treatment, it was another. It didn't help matters that two outsiders had descended on the office in a concentrated effort to locate some evidence. There was no way that the local field office was going to be responsible for any leaked investigative information. The word had already gone out that anyone caught talking to the press would be immediately suspended.

CHAPTER 24

ON THE DRIVE DOWN SOUTH, Vasili asked Pat to sit next to him in the front seat of the Van. He wanted Sam to have some privacy as he worked on compiling the software patches necessary to implement the plan.

"Are you going to tell me why you have me here?" Pat finally asked as the van passed through Columbus.

"I need your expertise with anatoxin-a."

A look of shock and disbelief flooded Pat's face, causing the capillaries to expand, turning his usually pinkish face a bright red.

"Do you know how dangerous that stuff is?"

"I know they call it 'Very Fast Death Factor' if that means anything to you."

"You can't be serious?" The enormity of his role was beginning to sink in. Vasili wanted his expertise with algae, in particular blue-green algae and the toxins that sometimes lived in the slime.

"I'm perfectly serious. It is ubiquitous, naturally occurring, and extremely toxic. I understand the death is painful, something akin to asphyxiation."

"I still don't get it. How to the two jobs link together?"

"On our way down south, you will isolate the toxin for me and breed a concentrated batch that will be loaded into a tank mounted on the drone. A simple modification, say something like a crop duster aspirator will put the toxin into aerosol form and dispensed from the drone as it flies over a populated area. No one will detect the aerosol until it is too late. The drone will be long gone by the time the toxin takes effect. If things work out, I may even collect the drone for a secondary mission. We will see how clever the US agents are and how fast they can react. I'm guessing I will have several drone missions before anyone catches on. You Americans are so ignorant. They're always looking in the wrong direction."

"And if I refuse to help?"

"Why pretend you have forgotten that I have little Jamie?"

Pat turned his head to the side window and watched the grass speed by. He could not live with either option, but could see no way out of the dilemma presented to him. The more he dwelt on the matter, the deeper he sunk into depression.

"Tell me, Mr. O'Connor, where would I find this infamous blue-green algae?"

"You mean the version of the anatoxin? It doesn't show up in all algae. It's easy to locate if you know what to look for, the telltale signs."

"Then you will assist me?"

"Do I have a choice?"

"See, you do understand. We all have choices. Just make sure you can live with yourself when you make them. And don't try to masquerade the toxin. They have informed me of a simple verification test."

After several side trips to various ponds and stagnant swamps, the material was located. Pat and Sam eventually collected enough material to fill a fifty-five-gallon drum that was put in the back of the van. Having that much toxic material in nearby made Pat as nervous as a cat. He was insistent on washing his hands several times before he would get back into the van. As a precaution, Vasili did the same even though Pat did all the collecting.

Now the plan was falling into place. The next stop was an abandoned airport in a secluded area of West Virginia. They hadn't quite hit the Appalachian Mountains when they approached their destination.

The air field was now more weeds than tarmac. In the distance, a light could be seen in a single farmhouse about a half mile away. Vasili pulled the van into the driveway of the farmhouse and walked up onto the porch and knocked on the door. An elderly man in his eighties opened the door.

"What do you want?"

Vasili pushed his way inside, then shot the man. The silencer he had put on his weapon let out only a muffled sound. Quickly, he dragged the man out the back door and into the barn. Vasili put a bit of hay over the body and made his way back to the van.

"We will stay here for the night. In the morning you can concentrate the toxin."

CHAPTER 25

SITTING IN HER MAKESHIFT OFFICE down the hall, Natasha complained, "I never should have agreed to this." She was used to the comfort of her office and this closet she was now using didn't suit her one bit.

"Any word yet about how much longer we need to hold them?"

"No."

"Can we at least move them?"

"I don't dare. That man is crazy. I've checked with my contacts in Bulgaria, he is not to be trifled with. No one is sure who he is or who he works for. They just know there are a lot of bodies on the ground when he leaves town. The word on the street is that when he was five, he slit the throat of the thirteen-year-old leader of a band of pickpockets because the lad tried to cheat him out of his cut. I'm not about to give him any excuse to question my support of whatever plan he has."

"That's the thing. We know nothing, why we have these women, what he plans to do with them or when?"

"I'll give you his number if you want to get some answers."

Markov raised both hands, shaking his head. Silently, he left the room to return to his post.

The frustration level was equally high for Jamie and Helen. They were allowed no newspapers, no radio, no television, nothing that would provide a glimpse of current events, a clue that someone, anyone, was looking for them.

Jamie was thinking of her family and the project she had left unfinished on her desk. She never even got to brief her boss about the changes that the client wanted. Now all she could do was dwell on how she might change things. She wasn't even allowed pen and pencil to write down her thoughts.

All they had to occupy their time was the books that lined the shelves in the office.

Natasha was well read and the book shelves reflected this. Works by authors such as Konstantinov, Todorov, Krastev, even Slaveykov and Vazov lined the walls behind the desk.

Jamie and Helen pulled down the books that were in English. Some they thumbed through, others like 'To Chicago and Back' they read. It passed the time and provided an insight into the thoughts of their captor. Not that they ever got the chance to debate the classics with the woman. Never once did Natasha show her face. The faces they saw all seemed to be low-ranking slumps. For all the women knew, they could be waitresses and dishwashers.

Helen took that as a good sign. Jamie wasn't so sure.

"Simply because we can't identify our captors doesn't mean they will allow us to live."

"Maybe not, but it provides me with a glimmer I can hang onto. In every television show I've ever seen, once the villain lets the victim see his face, that's the end for them."

There was, of course, no proper way to resolve the debate. They could only grasp onto things and hope somehow God would get them out of their present situation.

* * *

"Coop? I've deciphered who owned this laptop. The emails are to some guy named Ziar el Muhammad. He has links to Hamas's fund-raising activity, and he is on the 'No Fly List'. We've gotten no concrete evidence linking him to any criminal activity."

"You mean until now."

"Shall we pick him up?"

Patten grabbed his keys and headed out with his partner. Within thirty-five minutes, Ziar was sitting across a desk in the interrogation room. Ziar had lawyered up immediately and sat silently, waiting for counsel to arrive.

When he did, Wahhaaj Noor began citing Sharia law to the agents.

"We've been down that path before, Wahhaaj. None of that flies in this jurisdiction. Either stick to the US Code or get the heck out of here."

"Very well. What are you charging my client with?"

"Charging him? Who said anything about charges? We want to ask him a few questions about a computer of his we recovered."

"You broke into my client's house and stole personal property? I know you have no warrant, as you have not shown it to me or to my client. So, it must be theft. This keeps getting better. I'll have you both behind bars before nightfall."

"Don't get ahead of yourself. I did not take the computer from his house. We found it in a dumpster, presumably after he tried to get rid of it. We want to ask him a few questions."

"Ziar? Is this true?"

"I know nothing about any computer they think they have."

"Do you now or did you ever own an HP laptop?"

A momentary flash of recognition crossed Ziar's face as he brought to mind the computer he sold a few weeks earlier.

"It's not mine."

"So, you know what we have and what we found on it?"

"I know nothing of the sort."

"Let me refresh your memory. We reconstructed the hard drive and recovered the deleted emails detailing at least fifty-two illegal wire transfers to known terrorist organizations all in your name."

"My client is a fundraiser for widows and orphans in his native land. There is no crime in humanitarian efforts."

"The US Government doesn't share your view on that point, counselor. But today is your client's lucky day as we are more interested in the other data we found."

"What other data?"

"We found a copy of software that was stolen from the US Government last week."

Wahhaaj looked at Ziar. Ziar shook his head.

"It's not his data. He knows nothing about it."

"We can prove that the computer is his, and that he received stolen property."

"You mean you received stolen property and you are trying to frame an innocent, law-abiding citizen."

Coop knew the connection to Ziar was tenuous, but he needed to push. If there was a terrorist plot at the bottom of this, he needed to know the when and where.

"The software breach, combined with the illegal wire transfers, will be enough of a connection to put your client away for a long, long time. You know how the system works. From where I sit, it looks like guilt by association."

"The data's not mine. I told you. I sold that computer weeks ago to some infidel dog." Ziar barked.

"So, your memory is returning. And you say he was American? Do you know him?"

"No. He placed an ad, and I called him. We met near city hall and he paid cash. I never saw him before."

"Did you keep the phone number or the paper?"

"No, but the ad was in the Arab American Times, probably two, maybe three weeks ago. He specified the type of computer he wanted. It was very specific. He offered top dollar. I needed an upgrade anyway, so I thought, what's the harm?"

"What's the harm indeed? Can you describe him?"

"Tall, square-cut jaw, FBI haircut and shoes, bulging muscles between his ears. He looks like one of you."

CHAPTER 26

IN THE MORNING, VASILI took Pat out to the barn and helped him pull the barrel out of the van. From his studies of cyanobacterial blooms, Pat understood the mechanism that promoted the bloom of the anatoxin and he knew what factors limited its growth and caused it to degrade into less toxic substructures. It was his job to promote the one and limit the other until the concentration of the material was sufficient for whatever purpose Vasili had in mind.

Pat was conflicted. The problem was, he was never sure how sophisticated his adversary was in terms of his ability to check his work. Should he take the chance and destroy the toxin? What if Vasili found out? He couldn't run away and leave Sam there alone. It was a dilemma with no viable solution. In the end, he reluctantly decided to bide his time and follow orders hoping against hope that Sam wouldn't be able to complete his part of the operation or that the Air Force or someone would shoot down the drone before it reached whatever target Vasili had in mind.

Pat systematically went about working with the tools and chemicals available on the farm. They limited him in what he could do to promote the growth of the toxin, but he could take steps to prevent it from bio-degradation. He built a series of tubes that allowed the material to circulate across the ground and heat during the day. The pattern was not unlike he had developed in his fuel research. This would help the bacteria to self-propagate.

While he was waiting for the witches' brew to coalesce, Pat and Vasili began working on the aerosol distribution mechanism. A nozzle from a garden nose and a short length of hose would suffice. Vasili connected the hose to the water tap in the barn and adjusted the spray pattern to his satisfaction. The controlling mechanism would prove more difficult to construct.

The two looked around the barn searching for a suitable devise that could be used as a simple on-off switch. At first, Vasili thought the fuel pump from the tractor would suffice, but the design was from a mechanical pump, and that would be of no use. Then he realized there was a late model Pontiac in the driveway. He went to the house, got the keys, and drove the car into the barn. Vasili dropped the fuel tank. He unbolted the electric pump from the top of the tank and pulled it out of the tank along with a sufficient length of hose.

All they needed to do now was hard wire the pump to the drone and fashion a way to connect the two different diameter hoses. Then they would have an operational aerosol delivery system. It wasn't elegant, but it would be effective.

Sam spent his day in the farmhouse. He buried his nose in the computer screen. There were so many elements he needed to factor into the puzzle, so many patches he needed to write. It was all running together in his brain. All the little things he had considered, the elements that were necessary, some that were desirable, others he would get to if he got time. Time was something he had no control over. He didn't know what the time constraints were. He worked as fast as he could, hoping that it would somehow shorten the time until Helen would be released.

On a scratch pad next to the computer, he began prioritizing the list of changes. A spoof software patch, an algorithm to block any attempts to retake control, a weapon control mechanism to discharge the aerosol, a targeting system, a simplified interface to control everything requiring no specific skill set or knowledge by the operator.

Vasili would occasionally look over his shoulder and make notes on the priority list as to the elements he felt were essential. Sam would work on Vasili's priorities.

It took two long days and nights before the software was in a sufficiently robust form. Sam felt confident he could compile it. He ran through an emulator to simulate flight.

Vasili watched on the computer screen as the simulation mode took effect. They put the computer through several steps, take-off, flight, banking right and left, landing. Then they tried again with the weapons' discharge. Everything in the simulation worked as it was supposed to, and the streamlined interface seemed intuitive in its operation. Now Sam needed to upload it to the tablet and verify that it would still operate as intended. One step closer to the day he dreaded. What drove him was that it was also one day closer to the day they would release Helen, he hoped.

At first, the tablet version balked at the complexity of the command structure. Even though Vasili had procured a top of the line, full memory tablet, with the latest high-speed processor, Sam needed to take some actions to bypass the internal safety protocols in order to allow the various pieces of the software to communicate with each other. He had to cheat the system software, trick it into thinking the pieces were all part of a single software application before he could get it to operate successfully.

It took him two more days in order to get the tablet version working to his and Vasili's satisfaction. In the end, the simple elegance of the swipe and tap interface impressed Vasili, a man not easily impressed. This software would be extremely useful in the future for not only this, but for other applications. He would be the leader of the new world order of stealth warfare from half a continent away. This was everything that he had ever imagined, the answer to his prayer, that is if he in fact prayed. Already his mind was fast at work thinking through the next several assignments he would get, and how this new tool in his tool belt would simplify the task. Multiple versions could be copied and even a young boy with a high school education could now fly an airplane and become a pilot, firing missiles at whatever target he desired. The age of suicide bombers had ended.

Sam, for other reasons, was pleased with the final product. He, too, recognized its simple elegance. Now all the dominoes were stacking up nicely. Only the last one was necessary, the capstone, for the plan to be implemented.

CHAPTER 27

VASILI RAIDED THE CHICKEN COOP in the morning to get fresh eggs for breakfast. He made enough scrambled eggs for everyone. It was a day of celebration. Neither Pat nor Sam had much of an appetite. They picked at their food, moving it around on the plate.

The two close friends barely talked to each other. They directed their thoughts at those who were not in the room. Were they still safe? Were they being fed? Vasili refused to answer questions, but the implications from the constant threats led them to believe there was still hope.

"Mr. Kennedy? Are we a go on your end?"

"Things are as ready as I can get them."

"Mr. O'Connor? How many gallons of product do we have?"

"I estimate about one hundred. Whether that is sufficient, I have no way of knowing."

"Product? What are you talking about?" Sam looked at Pat for an answer.

"Mr. Kennedy, it is time I bring you further into the loop. When we commandeer the drone, I intend to have it used it in a crop-dusting mission of sorts."

Sam scrunched his face in a puzzled look. "I don't understand."

"The drone will distribute an aerosol on command. Is that sufficiently clear?"

"How do you plan on doing that? Where will you store the product? How will you control the drop zone and distribution? This is going to require more software patches and some hardware modifications. I'm not ready for this."

"No need to panic, my friend."

Sam glared at Vasili. You are not a friend; he thought.

"Mr. O'Connor and I have fashioned a nozzle and distribution system. We have an electric fuel pump you can mount on the drone and use as an on-off device. You need to write a 'patch'. Is that what you called it to control its operation?"

"It's not that simple. The pump you have isn't by chance an automotive fuel pump, is it?"

"Yes, what difference does that make?"

"The pump is twelve volts. I don't know the voltage of the drone, but most aviation systems operate at twenty-four volts. If the drone is not twelve volts, then I will have to build a transformer to convert the voltage or the pump will burn out."

"How long will that take?"

"I don't know. I don't have any of the components I would need. We're dead in the water."

"No. We're not. We've come too far. There is always a way. What are our options?"

"Options? There are no options."

"Come, come, you aren't forgetting my other guests, are you?"

And there it was, the unnecessary reminder of who was in control and how much control he had.

"You say we have a hundred gallons of liquid? What range do you require for this exercise?"

"Less than a thousand miles. Why?"

"Can we refuel before the mission?"

"Sure. We need to land it here anyway to load the product and make the modifications. What are you thinking?"

"There are two fuel tanks on the plane. We put the product in one and use the on-board fuel switching mechanism to trigger the release. Easy-peazy. We can use your nozzle and mount it to the tank outlet tube."

"So, we're back in business?"

"I think so, but it will take some time to modify the drone."

"We have another problem. We have a thirty-eight-hour window from the time the drone takes initial flight until it is due back. At that point all hell breaks loose when they discover one of their toys is missing." Vasili adds.

"Okay, thirty-eight hours, including flight time from the acquisition point to the target location, plus any detour for fuel, modifications, and anything else. How far from here are the acquisition and target locations?"

"Three hours at the most."

"Okay. We can work with that." Sam figured.

"Then we're back on track?"

"As soon as we get some Jet A and I will need a voltmeter."

"I'll drive down to the Sunoco station on the corner." Vasili was getting sarcastic with all these last-minute details. He was used to planning things out completely himself.

"This is Amish country. They'll have kerosene available. Will that work?"

"It's a good surrogate, especially if there is some residual fuel in the tank. Besides, if we are lucky, they will top the tanks off before they take off and we won't need additional fuel."

Sam's brain was operating at light speed now. It was never anything he could control or turn off once he started into problem-solving mode.

CHAPTER 28

IN THE MORNING VASILI loaded three fifty-five-gallon drums onto the bed of a stake truck he picked up the night before. He drove for an hour and a half to be sure none of the locals recognized the truck. He turned down a dirt road and drove several miles. On his left was an Amish farm that had a large kerosene tank. He pulled into the dirt path next to the house, climbed the stairs to the porch and knocked on the door, one hand on the Makarov that he kept behind his back. No one was home. As he walked around back, he could see two men in the field plowing behind a magnificent horse. They were at the far end of the field, headed away from him. A woman wearing a cotton dress and a bonnet approached him from the side of the house. She looked to be in her forties. Her arms filled with vegetables. She was startled that a visitor had come, but she flashed a smile of welcome. Vasili pulled his revolver out and fired a single shot. The muffled sound of the silencer was barely audible.

The vegetables spilled out onto the ground as the woman fell, her lifeless body collapsing onto the dirt behind the home. Only after the body hit the ground did Vasili notice the young girl of perhaps three or four that had been hidden behind the skirt of the woman. Vasili put a finger to his lips to tell the child to be quiet. He pointed at the vegetables and she began picking them up and putting them into a neat pile.

Vasili pulled his truck around back of the house where kerosene tank was located and began filling his drums. When he had finished filling the drums, he simply drove off.

As he passed through town, he picked up the other essentials Sam would need and then started back to the farm, confident that the plan was about to be put into effect.

* * *

"Pat? How bad is the product Vasili was talking about?"

"Its nickname is Very Fast Death Factor if that tells you anything."

"That bad? And you are sure of what you have?"

"Yes."

"Then we need to block the hose, prevent it from distributing the product."

"Sam please. Don't do anything stupid. Think of the women. I don't want any part of this anymore than you do, but I will not lose Jamie. If there is any chance of saving her, I've got to take it. No matter what the cost and you need to help me. I know deep down you feel the same about Helen. You would never forgive yourself if anything happened to her. I know, I know. The alternative is killing someone else, but maybe they deserve it. I'm sorry I didn't mean that. I'm having trouble processing all this." The anguish in Pat's voice was genuine.

"Alright Pat. I won't do anything stupid. But what if there was a way to disguise the spray or block his view of the spray so he couldn't verify it was being discharged? I could point the nozzle away from the ground camera. Would that be acceptable?"

"Sam, wouldn't he eventually find out that no one died?" Pat began pacing back and forth, nervous about the coming events.

"I guess you're right. Eventually, he would know. I'm afraid we're stuck."

Sam was of the same mindset as Pat when it came to saving the women. He would gladly sacrifice himself to save the other three if it came to that, but given the circumstances, it wasn't likely to come down to that point.

He knew Helen would forgive him for what he had to do and he felt strongly that Jamie would likely forgive Pat for his role. He wasn't so sure he could forgive himself.

In moral theology, there is the dilemma posed as a theoretical exercise in which a person faces two horrible choices, for example, stealing drugs that your mother needs in order to survive. The construct always allows for only these two choices, steal or death. There is no alternative. The debate centers on whether it is justified to do the one in order to prevent the other. Moral theologians differ on the outcome, the justification, and even the construct. Now, for Sam and Pat, the construct was all too real.

If only they could go back in time and erase the ridiculous thought exercise that they had. If only they could have not carried the conversation in a public place. They were too trusting. Now the one innocent statement had somehow cascaded into an avalanche of decisions, so not even the most eloquent theologian could find a justifiable solution.

Death was the only way out. Sam knew it. Pat probably did too. And they would spend what was left of their life regretting their role.

When Vasili returned with the supplies, Sam made the final arrangements. Everything was as set as it was going to be, at least until the drone arrived and they had to make the modifications.

CHAPTER 29

WHEN THE MORNING ARRIVED, a part of Sam was eager to try his new app. He wanted to know if it would work in real life. Was he good enough to do the job? His stomach was in a knot. The thought of failure scared the hell out of him.

If he wasn't good enough, would Helen be dead before lunch? The thought was paralyzing. His hand shook as he tapped the icon to launch the drone app. The program opened. So far, so good. He tapped on the menu and launched the acquisition application. The screen shifted to a satellite view of the terrain. There were no drones visible within five hundred miles. He placed his thumb and forefinger on the screen and pushed them apart in order to get a wider view. A single red dot appeared over Lake Ontario, headed towards Maine.

"I see only one available drone at the moment. I have no idea how long it has been in the air. Shall I acquire it?" Sam was ambivalent at this point. It no longer mattered to him what happened next.

"Go ahead."

Now came the moment of truth. Could his algorithm really acquire a live drone? A few screen taps later and the red dot turned green. The current readings from the machine appeared on the screen. Sam couldn't help but smile.

"Things look fine. The fuel level is over three-quarters full, so it must have taken off relatively recently. Shall I continue?"

"Yes, yes, of course." Vasili was anxiously peering over Sam's shoulder.

Working quickly, Sam tapped on the file locater and with his finger scrolled through the list of mission logs saved on the drone's computer. He selected one from the previous week, hoping that the pattern would be the same. He queued it up and recognized the ground sequence. Working quickly, he aligned the file to the current location.

"I am selecting the spoof file now. We can only hope there are no deviations from the previous mission." There was a momentary blip on the screen as the spoof file loaded. The location seemed to be the same to Sam's eye, so he flipped the screen to live mode. "Okay, here we go. I am giving the drone a command to fly to our location." He issued a command to send the drone south by putting his finger on the drone and dragging it down the screen. The drone responded to the new set of commands and banked to the right.

The scenery from the camera showed the drone headed south.

On a separate screen, he watched the spoof signal that was being sent back to the operator. All he could do was hope that the operator didn't issue any unanticipated deviations.

"Okay. Now we wait and see if anyone tries to take command back."

Sam dragged the drone down to the 'x' on the screen that marked his current location. There was nothing to do at that point except wait. It would take the drone approximately one hour and thirty-five minutes to reach the airfield.

The three men waited at the farmhouse until about fifteen minutes before the drone arrived, and then Sam and Vasili headed over to the abandoned airstrip. Pat was in the barn loading the drums onto the stake truck, getting ready for his part.

When everything was ready, Vasili got behind the wheel. Sam and Pat sat beside him. All was quiet on the short drive. The stake truck parked on one end of the field next to an old hangar. Vasili opened the doors and drove the truck inside the hangar. There was no sense in taking chances someone would drive by.

As the drone approached, Sam tapped on the landing app and put the UAV into automatic pilot. He entered the designated coordinates, and the machine took over for a perfect landing. Sam retook manual control and guided the drone into the hangar, then shut it down.

The three men walked around the machine, examining the details. Looking over to where the fuel tanks were located and examining the maintenance hatches. There was plenty to do now, and they were under a time constraint.

The first job was to drain the excess fuel from the secondary tank. They transferred as much fuel as they could to the primary, then let the rest drain onto the ground. Pat rigged a pump system and loaded the toxin into the secondary fuel tank. Sam busied himself with the drain hose that would serve as a distribution nozzle. Vasili positioned the nozzle below the vehicle out of the way of the landing gear.

Sam opened the maintenance hatches and examined the flight gear. He located the switching mechanism for the secondary tank and cut into the line immediately after the junction. With a clamp and an old bolt, he closed off the live end of the fuel drain tube that led to the primary fuel tank, then tucked this length of hose out of the way.

"I need a longer piece of hose if we are to connect it to the nozzle location you have. Vasili, can you see if there is anything we can use in the back room?"

Vasili wasn't used to being ordered around, but he knew more than anyone there was a time crunch. Reluctantly, he went in search of the tubing. It seemed more efficient than having Sam interrupt his work every time he needed a tool or a part.

"Pat, can you reach the volt meter? I need to verify the voltage."

Pat handed the tool to Sam and waited for the next assignment. He was not as mechanically inclined as Sam, but he knew his way around a toolbox.

"There's nothing back here. Now what?"

Sam thought for a minute. "Can you drive back to the barn and pick up the fuel line from the tractor? And bring the garden hose just in case. Better to have more than we need then to make multiple trips."

The trip to the barn and back took only twenty minutes and when Vasili returned, he handed Sam the fuel line, which was too short, then he handed the garden hose. Sam cut a length and with two clamps, and made the necessary connections.

"Now we see if it works." Sam grabbed the tablet and tapped on the screen to bring up the fuel panel. A few quick taps, and he opened the secondary line that would transfer fuel to the primary tank. Immediately, the liquid started spraying out the nozzle onto the ground.

"Careful with that stuff. It's poison." Vasili shouted as he jumped away from the splashing liquid.

Sam tapped on the screen and turned off the pump.

"Well, at least we know it works."

CHAPTER 30

THE MOMENT HAD FINALLY ARRIVED. Conditions were not ideal for flying. There was a low ceiling and a chance of rain off to the west. Sam tapped the app to open it, then went into the take-off menu. A few more taps and the powerful turbine whirled to life, shaking the surrounding ground. Vasili could feel his own adrenaline rush through his veins, coursing through his muscles, inching through his neural network. His entire life he had wanted revenge on America, on Americans, for what they had done to his parents. Now he was seconds away.

Sam taxied the drone to the runway and pointed the nose into the wind. A few more taps, and the drone was airborne. Sam guided the drone to an altitude of ten thousand feet.

"What now?" he turned towards Vasili, waiting for the location he would send the drone.

"Set the initial destination for sixteen hundred Pennsylvania." Vasili replied.

Sam looked at him in disbelief. "The toxic chemicals can't move through walls."

"I know. I'm just making a point. And who knows, if some of the material makes its way into the air handling system, so much the better."

Sam shook his head, then tapped in the coordinates. "Everything is set." This doesn't make any sense, Sam thought. After all this planning, he has to know about the no-fly zone.

"You won't get within fifty miles." Sam offered, knowing his comments weren't likely to be heeded.

"When you are one hundred miles out, I want you to drop to treetop level. It will limit the distribution area, but it will neutralize your Air Force. They won't dare risk firing on us at that altitude. Not over a populated area."

Now it was making more sense.

Pat looked at Sam, hoping the Air Force would somehow track the plane early before it went over the populated area. He regretted telling his friend not to do anything stupid.

"Are there any on-board jamming devices?" Vasili asked, looking at the tablet screen.

"Yeah, I think I saw something on the weapons console." Sam clicked over to the next menu.

"Here it is. I thought I remembered seeing it before. I have activated it."

As the plane made its way across the landscape, a green dot was clearly visible on the monitor, moving at what seemed like a snail's pace across the tablet screen. If the green dot disappeared, that meant that the drone had been destroyed. Pat kept praying that the little green dot disappeared.

In the navigation panel, Sam tapped in the command to reduce altitude. The plane began responding to the command, then he used his two fingers to zoom in on the location, providing a finer grid on the tablet. The visual image from the camera pointed to the ground showed recognizable landmarks as it heading across the Potomac.

CHAPTER 31

COOPER AND PATTEN WERE GETTING nowhere with their investigation. They knew they had the right computer; they found the hack used to gain access. What they didn't have was the hacker. They brought Ziar back in, this time without his lawyer. They were not there to accuse him. Today they wanted Ziar to sit down with a Police sketch artist. For the time being, they wanted to follow up on his story and try to track down the mystery man.

Six other citizens from the Dearborn area, all of Arabic decent, had sold computers to the person, or persons, who placed the ad. The problem was there was no crime linked to any of the other computers. Ziar's was the only one. He was smug when he sat down with the artist. He joked the artist should sketch Patten. The artist never even smiled. Neither did Patten nor Coop. It took an hour and a half of back and forth, sketch and erase, before the artist's sketch satisfied Ziar.

As the artist turned the sketch around to show the agents, someone rushed through the door to the sketch room.

"You have to see this." The agent shouted, motioning for everyone to follow him into the bullpen area where a television monitor was hanging from the ceiling.

Coop, Patten, Ziar, and the artist all walked out of the sketch room into the bullpen area. The artist was still holding the sketch book at his side.

On the television screen was live coverage of a drone flying over the Nation's capital.

Coop and Patten looked at Ziar for any reaction. Knowing that he was being watched, Ziar's reaction was cautious, not at all his normal, snarky self.

"I'm so sorry. I never realized this was so serious. I pray to Allāh that no one gets hurt today." His tone was sincere, almost caring.

* * *

Natasha was sitting at the small desk in her makeshift office down the hall from her guests. It was necessary to keep the two women in her office as it was at the end of the hall and provided a more secure location, one that was more difficult to break out of.

As she busied herself with the routine of restaurant manager, she had the television turned to the news. When she heard the 'breaking news' announcement, she stopped her bookkeeping and looked up at the monitor.

"Vasili," she said out loud. She recognized his hand in the drone that was headed straight for the White House. She shook her head. Well, it will all be over in a matter of a few minutes, she thought. Then I will get the word on what to do with the women.

The idea of getting her office back pleased her, but she had work to do. She needed to plan for the contingency to get rid of two bodies.

CHAPTER 32

THE PRESIDENT WAS SITTING on the couch in his office, reading the sports page. His half-finished cup of coffee poured into the Truman China cup sat on the table next to him when the Secret Service rushed in.

"We have an incident, Mr. President. We need to get you into the box."

"What happened?"

"A bogey has entered the restricted airspace near the White House. We need to get you out of here NOW."

"My family?"

"Already headed down." The secret service agent grabbed the President's arm and quickly escorted him from the room.

"Have we scrambled the fighters?" Sensing the urgency, the President began jogging alongside of the agent.

"Yes. The Air Force Tactical Command has jets in the air, but they have not been authorized to fire over civilian terrain. Do you wish to give that command?"

"No, let's get to the situation room first. I want to see this for myself."

As they entered the secure bunker somewhere deep in the bowels of the West Wing, the six flat panel monitors were already alight with visuals of the aircraft headed straight for the

White House. The Security Council staff assembled at their posts and the intelligence team gathered even before the President arrived. There were many questions that needed answers and not enough answers to suit any of the advisers.

"What is that thing? It looks like one of ours."

"It is. It is a MQ-9 unmanned aerial vehicle."

"A drone? Who's in command of that thing?"

"We don't know."

"Well, find out."

"We had an F-117 do a flyby and pick up the tail number. It belongs to ICE. They report that they have the command."

"What the hell do they think they are doing buzzing the White House? I want someone's butt."

"That's the strange thing." The General tapped the computer in front of him.

"This is the live feed from their computer. They think the drone is somewhere over Maine."

"What?"

"The drone has been stolen, Sir. Someone else is in charge of the thing."

"Are you certain?"

"Captain Greyson, are you there?"

"Yes sir."

"This is General Montgomery at Tactical Command authenticy code Alpha-Gamma-niner-five-five-seven. Do you authenticate?"

"Yes, Sir."

"I want you to execute a ninety-degree turn to starboard now."

"Banking right. What the?"

"Is there a problem, Captain?"

"Sir, I executed the command, but the drone didn't respond. It is maintaining its course and heading."

"Thank you, Captain. That will be all for now."

"Well, we're certain now."

"Can we reestablish control?"

"We don't dare execute the self-destruct sequence, not over the Capital."

"Captain Greyson, I want you to reboot your system and try to regain control of the drone. Report when you have control. Acknowledge."

"Yes, Sir. Rebooting now." Greyson responded to the request as he hurriedly tried to reestablish control using his secondary command console.

"What are our options?" The urgency in the President's voice made it sound higher pitched than usual.

"We can't very well follow it at treetop level, not at that speed. Our fighters would scare the hell out of everyone in the city. We will continue to monitor it. Our reconnaissance images show that it is not armed. So, we wait and see what's on his mind. When it gets into an area that is unpopulated, we can take other measures to destroy it. That is, if it hasn't pulled a nine-eleven by then."

"A nine-eleven?" the President didn't immediately comprehend the reference.

"Crash into a building, sir."

Everyone's eyes focused on the surveillance footage on the big screen in the front of the war room as the drone passed over the White House and headed across the National Mall towards the Capital. Off to the side of the main screen were the live feeds from the networks. ABC, CBS, FOX, even Al-Jazeera were streamed into the situation room. Every feed was tracking and commenting on the events as they were unfolding.

"We need to clear the Capital," the President commanded.

"We're trying, sir. There are too many people in there to get them all out in time."

"Then let's hope to God that isn't the target." The uncertainty of what would happen next was setting everyone on edge.

Silence filled the room as everyone held their breath. Memories of the World Trade Center coming down were flooding the brains of those in the room as they watched—seconds passed. Every tick of the clock seemed like an eternity. The drone was now directly over the Capital. It passed a few feet above the dome, then continued off to the east. There was a collective sigh of relief across the situation room.

That sigh was short-lived as the drone began making a hundred eighty-degree turn preparing to make a second run at the Federal City.

"Here we go again. This may be it."

"Sir, do you want to take it out?"

The President stood silent, staring at the screen in disbelief. There was no good option.

"Sir? If you want to deploy, now is the time."

"No. Do not deploy. Can we tell what it is doing? Can it be dropping something?"

"Impossible to say, given the climatics. I think it is going to be used as a tactical weapon itself."

"Just how much damage can it do?"

"Well, that depends on what it hits. The thing is small, as far as aircraft go. It weighs about the same as an SUV. But it carries four thousand pounds of fuel when fully loaded. The major damage will be from the fire. We have the fire department standing by, just in case."

"Any luck on reestablishing control?"

DRONE

"Negative, Captain Greyson has rebooted his system and he cannot reestablish control. We are working on the problem."

"This thing isn't on a joy ride. It seems to have some mission in mind."

"Yes, sir. But what?"

The President shrugged his shoulders and shook his head.

CHAPTER 33

"WE'RE HERE LIVE REPORTING from the steps of the Capital where moments ago a US Military Drone flew over the building. The aircraft, shown now on your screens at home, passed over the White House and the National Mall and is now headed out over the Atlantic. Bret? What is the reaction you're hearing?"

"Thanks Melissa. The reaction to what is a clear political stunt is outrage. Senate Democrats are reacting negatively to what is being called an unacceptable endangerment of lives for blatant political purposes. Members of the Senate Armed Services Committee are in a closed meeting and were unavailable for comment on who is behind this stunt. But I can tell you that tensions are rising and the finger pointing has already begun. Back to you, Melissa."

"The reaction from environmentalists has been swift and harsh, calling for a ban on all military aircraft within the DC airspace. We take you now to Environmental Defense headquarters for a live interview."

"With me is Michele Donovan, the chief spokesperson. Michele, what is your reaction to the events we have witnessed today?"

"Like all peace-loving people, it angered me to see this blatant waste of national resources above our Nation's capital.

The hawks on the Hill should be ashamed of themselves for this brazen display. The pollution alone is an unacceptable risk to the public. Many people have been calling our offices to report actually seeing pollution emanating from the aircraft. The emissions from that aircraft expose tens of thousands of Washingtonians to hazardous carcinogens. We need to put a stop to this RIGHT NOW."

"Melissa? Sorry to interrupt, but only moments ago they informed me that the drone is banking and appears to be ready to make another pass over the Capital. We have our traffic helicopter standing by with a live camera feed. You can see the plane headed back over the center of the city where the seat of our nation's government stands."

"That's amazing Bret. And we still have no word on who is behind this stunt?"

"That's right Melissa. We still do not have any official confirmation."

"Is there any possibility that this is a terrorist attack?"

"Word from our sources in the Pentagon is that there is no way for a terrorist group to gain control of a military drone. And our own visual observation confirms the drone is unarmed. We have asked repeatedly if the military is missing any aircraft and the word we are hearing is that no military or civilian drones are being reported missing."

"There you have it. We can see the drone coming into view again. It appears as if it will not make a second pass over the Capital or the National Mall but appears to be headed north of that area away from the primary group of civilians who always congregate on the Mall this time of day."

"We can see the drone clearly passing a few blocks north of the Mall now. It is headed in a westerly direction over the Judiciary Square area and back towards the Pentagon. We will continue to monitor the events as they unfold live from our Nation's capital."

CHAPTER 34

AFTER THE DRONE PASSED over the Pentagon, Vasili ordered it to head West North West up the George Washington Memorial Parkway towards Langley. This was the target that meant the most to him. It was the first time that he wished he had procured a weapons kit so that he could take a few shots at the George Bush Center for Intelligence.

He focused his eyes on the screen in front of him. There was no tail camera, so he couldn't verify that the Marine helicopters were tracking the progress, waiting for an opportunity to take down the wildcat drone. Still flying at treetop level, any shot would certainly result in collateral damage to those driving on the parkway.

Sam couldn't help but wonder what the military was waiting for. Why would they hesitate to take the shot? What was stopping them? Maybe they couldn't tell what was happening. Maybe they couldn't, with any certainty, know whether the drone was friend or foe. He had taken no shots, fired no weapons. Clearly, there were not even any weapons on-board. The only thing he could conclude was that the Military somehow wanted to regain control of the drone or at a minimum follow it back to its point of origin. Certainly, by now they had determined from the call numbers painted on the side who the vehicle belonged to. Maybe the military had even tracked the hack that had obtained the command control software. Sam couldn't help but wonder if they would track the hack back to him. What had Vasili done with that computer he used? Had he planted it somewhere for the police to find with evidence that would link to him? There were too many questions flooding into his consciousness like a damn had burst.

His thoughts were not only for himself, he worried about his beloved Helen. Would she forever be known as the next Marina Oswald? The bitterness of that thought consumed him. How could he have gotten himself into this situation? Would anyone ever explain his side of the story, see it from his point of view? Would he ever be able to tell Helen how much he loved her?

CHAPTER 35

"SIR, THE UAV HAS CROSSED over the Pentagon. This may be an aerial reconnaissance mission. It has flown over several strategic targets and hasn't yet attacked any of them. We can only assume at this point that it is a test of our defenses. It is trying to determine how we will react."

"We haven't reacted." The President responded in dismay. Everyone in the Situation Room shared his feeling of helplessness and frustration. "How could this have happened? And why can't we regain control?"

"We're working on the problem, Sir. Do you want to give the command to attack? We have Angel Squadron in the air and they are in position." General Montgomery sensed the President wanted to take action.

"No. The probability of civilian casualties is too high. That thing has to land sometime and when it does, I want it back, understand?"

"Yes, sir." The General was as anxious as his commanding officer to end this embarrassment. He gave the order to Angel Squadron to follow and commandeer the UAV when it landed.

"Sir, the UAV had passed over Langley and is now changing direction. Its new vector will put it over Reston shortly."

"What could it possibly want there? I recall nothing of strategic importance in that area?" The President scrunched up his face as if deep in thought.

"At this point, we cannot be sure that is his target. The flight path is getting more unpredictable with each passing minute."

"And as far as we can tell, there are no casualties, nothing was dropped from the drone?"

"That's correct, Sir. No casualties, nothing dropped that we can detect."

"What is on his mind? Could he be returning the vehicle to where it came from? Could it be that simple? Some clown wanted to prove it could be done, so he stole a drone and now wants to return it?"

"Sir, I honestly don't know. The initial point of departure from its last known point of control suggests that it was taken from somewhere over Lake Ontario. It would have to make a ninety-degree turn to get back home. We will continue to monitor its progress. Sir, do you want me to clear the airspace? It seems we have a number of civilian helicopters following Angel Squadron."

"Negative. Not unless we witness a hostile action. Then we need to take that thing down." Finally, the President gave some direction that the military could understand and act on.

CHAPTER 36

PAT, HIS HANDS TIED BEHIND his back, wept in anguish at the thought that he had killed countless innocent victims. He could never forgive himself, nor, he suspected, could Jamie ever forgive him. Far too many times he had forgotten to say I love you to that woman. Far too many times had he done some inconsiderate act and asked for forgiveness. Now he couldn't even think how he could ask or if he would ever be given the chance.

Vasili smiled at the loss of life that he considered worthless.

Sam knew what was coming next. He looked over at his friend, helpless to do anything. He only hoped to keep Vasili talking.

"Where do you want the drone to go now? Is there another target you have in mind?"

"I don't care. The American military will eventually target the drone and destroy it, but I hold the key to the future with the software you are holding in your hands. I can recreate this event whenever and wherever I want. Give it to me."

Sam realized he was the next target. He pleaded with Vasili to let his wife and Jamie live.

"Let the women go free. They are of no use to you. They haven't seen you, can't identify you. I give you my word they won't give you away if only you will let them live."

Vasili's eyes focused on Sam. "Give me the tablet," he demanded.

Sam handed over the object that was hanging at his side. Vasili examined it, swiped the screen, and tapped the icons. Nothing seemed to work.

"What have you done? Why can't I control the drone? You have locked me out. I should kill you now. But no, better I shoot your friend first. Then I will let you listen while I have your wife killed."

"No, wait. Don't do anything. There is a failsafe mechanism built into the software as a precaution. If no commands are issued for ten minutes, the software defaults to autopilot and the screen locks. I did this to prevent the system from falling into the hands of others."

"How do I get control back?" Vasili was growing impatient. He needed the software more than he needed Sam.

"You need to enter the passcode. On the top left is the menu. Tap that icon. When the system is in default mode, that will open the keypad. Type in 846-24-12." Sam repeated the code number slowly as he watched Vasili enter the code.

"Once you plug in the code, you will have access to all the functions. As long as you send at least one command every ten minutes, you will not have to reenter the pass code. Do you understand? Are you a pilot?"

"No, but I can get this to those who are. Walk me through how to acquire a drone."

"Tap the menu icon. Do you see the seek option at the top? When you tap it, the screen will change and you will be in acquire mode. The software will locate any drone within five hundred miles. Use your thumb and forefinger in an expanding motion on the screen if you need to see a wider area. Those little red dots are drones. The green one is the one you currently control. Tap on any red dot and you will see its command structure flight information on a separate screen. Taking control is a little tricky. You need to hack into the command sequence. This will give you access to everything, including the memory module, where you can pick the 'spoof' sequence to deceive the 'on the loop' operator. At that point, you have control. The other icons control the various functions." Sam patiently walked Vasili through the various functions, take-off, landing, flight, weapons. "Now I have told you everything. I don't care what you do with me. Promise me you will not harm the women."

"Oh, I will kill you. I will also kill your women."

Vasili pointed the Makarov at Sam. He smiled then, thanked him for his cooperation...

There was a flash.

Vasili stood looking at the sky. His chest burned as he fell to the ground. The tablet, no longer in his hand, lay shattered on the ground from the burst of light.

"What happened?" The shock from the flash was clear on Pat's face.

Sam walked over to his friend.

"As a precaution, I modified the targeting laser, increased its power, and changed the frequency to emit a wide spectrum. High frequency burst at a wavelength that... well, you saw what it did. The code he entered activated the sequence, and the drone targeted the tablet and whoever was holding it."

A fraction of an instant later, there was a mid-air explosion as the laser overheated, causing the drone to explode. Reflexively, both Sam and Pat ducked their heads into their shoulders.

As Sam removed the rope that bound Pat's hands, he explained. "You don't have to worry about the bacteria either. The heat from the explosion no doubt destroyed all of it."

"Not all of it. What about the amount that went over Washington?" The sadness in his voice was palpable.

"Pat, I did something else stupid. I only spoofed the control that opened the valve. I never released the bacteria."

Pat reached over and embraced his friend, his body trembling as he sobbed in relief.

CHAPTER 37

"MELISSA, WE HAVE AN UPDATE on Dronegate. In a strange twist of events, the drone that flew over the Nation's capital earlier today has crashed somewhere in West Virginia. Several news choppers and military attack helicopters were flying behind the drone when it mysteriously exploded. We have video footage that was shot by Channel Four's traffic copter. Our helicopters were not fast enough to keep up with the drone, so I apologize in advance for the quality of the footage, as it is a bit grainy. You can see ahead of our camera that there are six military helicopters chasing the drone when suddenly—stop the footage—the drone explodes. We could not determine if the military helicopters fired on the drone or if it experienced a mechanical failure. Our crews are on the way to the crash scene. We will break in with updates as the situation develops."

* * *

"Bret, I'm being told we have an update on Dronegate."

"That's right, Melissa. It is being reported that the National Transportation Safety Board is on its way to the crash site. In a separate report by an affiliated network, we have an as yet unconfirmed piece of information that the military police have staked off the area and are not allowing reporters or camera crews within the crash radius. We do not know how far they will keep us away. Our contacts in the Pentagon cannot confirm the reports that there are military police on site or if they are in route. We believe this may be a precaution in case of a fire from the jet fuel aboard."

"Bret, is there any word on who was commanding the drone?"

"No, Melissa, we still have no official word. Indications are that the drone was assigned to the Immigration and Customs Enforcement Operation, a branch of the Department of Homeland Security. What it was doing in the Washington area is still a mystery. It could be related to the upcoming Congressional hearings on Immigration reform but that is mere speculation at this point."

CHAPTER 38

"SIR, WE HAVE A DEVELOPMENT." General Montgomery pointed to the screen.

The President looked up at the monitor in the front of the room. The flash of the explosion was still clear. "What happened? Did we do that?"

The general tapped the call button on the panel in front of him. "Angel Leader, this is General Montgomery. Did you attack?"

"Negative, sir."

"Do we know what happened?" The General knew everyone would need some quick answers.

"Sir, we witnessed the targeting laser on the UAV activate moments before the explosion. We could not ascertain the target, somewhere west of our current position. Seconds later, the UAV exploded. It must have been a malfunction in the targeting system, Sir."

"I want the crash site secure. No reporters, and no curious civilians, understand? I will send a recovery team. Collect every bolt from that damn thing. I want to know what went wrong."

"Sir, yes, Sir."

"Airman, get me Quantico. I want the base commander. And get me Major General Waverly at Anacostia."

"Sir, I have Lieutenant General Westmoreland on line one."

"Wes, Montgomery here. I want you to send a battalion to the site of the UAV that crashed. Contact Angel Squad to get the exact coordinates. I want the area secured within the hour and I want every scrap of material from that thing located, catalogued, and returned. Understand."

"Yes, Sir."

"Sir, General Waverly is holding on line two."

"John, this is Montgomery. Listen, I have a bit of a strange one for you. Have you been watching the incident over the Capital?"

"Can't help but watch it. Everyone is wondering what clown would pull such a stunt. For his sake, I hope he isn't one of ours."

"We have a report from Angel Squadron that the MQ-9 targeted a site somewhere west of the DC area, within a couple of hundred miles. I can't be more specific. I want you to search for the site and secure it. We need to find out who they were targeting and why."

"It's not much to go on, but we'll get on it. Who else is tied in?"

"At the moment, Westmoreland is securing the crash site. Maybe he can uncover the information from the targeting computer. Keep me informed. Montgomery out."

"Mr. President? Is there anything else you would like us to do?" The General did all he could from a military standpoint.

"I want Homeland Security kept in the loop. At the moment, I don't want them taking the lead, in case it was an inside job. Pete, I hope you understand, it's nothing personal. The FBI will be the primary investigative arm once we have concluded the operator was not one of ours. The Bureau may already be on this for all I know. Someone had to get the command software from somewhere either within the US or from one of our allies. We need to find the source of the leak and plug it fast. And I want a complete briefing from Justice at three. Are we agreed we can leave the bunker now?"

CHAPTER 39

SAM REACHED DOWN AND SEARCHED Vasili's pockets. He pulled out his smart-phone.

"We need to get out of here and find Helen and Jamie." Sam opened the list of contacts on the phone. There were none. He went to the recent call list and saw several calls to a phone number in the two-one-two area code. He pushed resend.

"Vasili?" the voice on the other end answered. "I saw the video coverage; you have been busy. I suspect our dealings are ending. What do you want me to do with my guests?"

Sam looked at Pat, who was close enough to hear the conversation. Pat opened his mouth to say something, but Sam put his finger to his mouth to silence the conversation.

Doing his best to imitate Vasili's brusque style, he said into the phone, "release them."

"What, you can't be serious? After all..."

Sam turned to Pat again, not knowing how to communicate the urgency of the request.

In the delay that occurred over the phone line, the voice on the other end, after a lengthy pause, replied, "Vasili, I'm sorry. I didn't mean to question you or your methods. Please don't be angry with me. I will do as you request. Today. I will take them to a location far from here, one that won't track back to you or to us. Before noon today I will leave them at the Central Park North station. Forgive me Vasili, please?" There was genuine fear in the woman's voice.

Sam tapped end. "Central Park North? That sounds like a subway stop. Do you think they might be in New York?"

"I think so. Do you still have the laptop?" Pat asked.

They walked back to the stake truck and searched through the bags behind the driver's seat. There were three laptops.

The two friends drove back to the farmhouse and tried to connect to the Internet. They couldn't locate any signal. Their only hope was to find a Wi-Fi connection. But where? They were in rural West Virginia. They got back into the truck and wound their way north and east on a series of winding country roads. Eventually, they reached highway one-nineteen and the town of Grafton.

They didn't dare talk to the police in the small town, no telling what the police would do if they tried to explain their story. Sam located an internet connection and confirmed there was a Central Park North subway station in New York City.

"Pat, I think it best that we go to the FBI and have them locate the girls. What do you think?"

"Yeah, sure. Do you have the number?"

Sam dialed the number he found online and gave the agent who answered the information he had about the expected drop off location for the two kidnap victims. He didn't want to go into details on the phone about the other events, but promised to follow up with the agent later in the day. There was no need to give the agent his number.

"You're thinking of turning yourself in, aren't you?" Pat asked, noting the look in Sam's eye.

"I think it best. It is the only way we can clear our name. We are the victims here, but we need to convince other people about

143

what happened. The nearest FBI field office is in Pittsburgh. I can drop you off somewhere. You don't have to get involved if you don't want."

Pat eyed his friend, then put his arm around Sam's shoulder as he ushered him back to the truck. "Buddy, we started this together and we'll finish it together."

It took two hours to find their way up interstate seventy-nine to the field office. When they arrived, they parked the truck in the visitor's parking lot and walked in the front door. The guard at the front stopped them and asked, "Can I help you?"

"Yes, sir," Pat said politely. "We have some information on that drone that flew over the Capital earlier today."

The guard looked at them in disbelief, then made a few phone calls. After a few minutes, they ushered Sam and Pat to a conference room on the second floor. Someone already assembled several agents in the room.

Sam took a step back as he saw the look on the agents' faces. Pat put his hand on Sam's shoulder, "Let's get this over with."

The conversation started in somewhat reverse chronological order with the dead body. Once the location had been established, the Special Agent in Charge called down to the team on site at the crash and sent them to Roy Airfield in West Virginia to collect the body. That was step one.

The next conversation related the phone call they made to the FBI about the kidnapped women. Sam handed over Vasili's phone, which the SAIC gave to the technician, who walked out of the room to examine it for other clues. Sam and Pat were both eager to learn if anyone had collected Helen and Jamie yet.

"Yes, both women are safe. We have them in the New York office. You can talk to them later. They are reasonably well, a bit dingy from the ordeal but unharmed. I'm told they are cleaning up a bit."

"That's comforting." Sam added.

"We are debriefing them on what they know about their abductors and where they were held. From what I can gather so far, they don't know much, only that they were kept somewhere in New York that was noisy at night. They couldn't tell us the location because their heads were covered when they left the building."

As the day passed into evening, Sam and Pat related the details of their own kidnapping and their forced role in the drone's acquisition, the bio-hazard that was put onboard and how they escaped their captor. The agents were particularly interested in the hacking and how three men could circumvent the security protocols of the Defense Department.

Sam patiently went through the details several times. It was a complicated process, and the agents were not particularly well versed in computer code. Finally, Sam reached into the bag he brought with him and handed over the laptop with the code. "You'll find it all in here."

At that point, a voice on the speakerphone spoke up.

"This is Agent Cooper. I'm with the cyber-security task force. Can you tell me if the computer you have belongs to you?"

"No, it does not." Sam replied.

"Do you know where it came from?"

"Nope. Vasili gave us this computer."

"Did he ever give you other computers?"

"Yes. After he kidnapped us, he handed us a different computer. That was the one I used to hack into NASA to get the control software." Sam offered.

"And do you still have that computer?"

"No sir. I don't know what happened to it. After I completed the hack, I was told to transfer the software to a different computer. At that point, Vasili took the first computer from me.

I don't know what he did with it. Nor can I tell you where we were. I know we were close to where we were kidnapped. We were in a warehouse somewhere and we piggybacked on an internet signal from a nearby cafe or restaurant or something."

"Thank you, Mr. Kennedy. That clears up a few questions I have." Coop remarked.

"I don't understand?"

"The computer is in our possession. We found it smashed and dumped in a trash bin behind a Hookah lounge in Dearborn. We tracked down the owner of the computer and he denied any involvement in the software theft."

"Like I said, I don't know where the computer came from or where it ended up. But the man you have is likely innocent. I doubt Vasili would have used a computer from someone associated with him. He seemed very careful, very deliberate in his planning." There was weariness in Sam's voice.

"Are we done here? I'd like to go to New York and see my Jamie." Pat added. He, too, wanted the ordeal to be over.

"I think so. We have your home contact information. I would suggest you not leave the country for a while. We may have more questions for you later. If you like, we can fly you to New York or if you prefer, we can fly you and your spouse's back to Detroit. Your choice."

Pat and Sam looked at each other. "Detroit," they both said simultaneously.

CHAPTER 40

WHEN THE FBI JET LANDED IN DETROIT, Sam and Pat were met by agents Cooper and Patten. The agents escorted into a room in one of the private hangars along Merriman Road. The hangar was small, with a capacity for five or six executive class business jets. Inside the hangar were three conference rooms. The group entered the room closest to the hangar area.

Once everyone was seated, Agent Cooper pulled out a smashed computer from his duffel bag and showed it to the men.

"Is this the computer you used?"

Sam examined the computer. "It seems to be the same one. Of course, when I saw it last, the computer wasn't damaged. Were you able to get anything useful from it?"

"Yes, we now know the security hole you breached, and we have recovered the command software. You say there was another computer involved?"

"That's right. The Agent in Pittsburgh has it now."

"So, you controlled the drone from the other laptop?"

"No, not exactly. I used the other computer to write the patches I needed. I transferred the software to a tablet. It was more portable and had a four-g connection. We could communicate from almost anywhere. It seemed easier. I cloned a signal processor in order to convert the frequency to a UHF signal and bounced it off cell towers until it found an antenna in close enough proximity to the actual drone."

"And what did you do with the tablet?"

"It was destroyed. You can find the pieces on the ground next to our kidnapper in West Virginia."

"Is the software app recoverable?"

Sam shrugged his shoulders. He never really gave it any thought. "You still have the computer in Pittsburgh, don't you? I can build you a version from that. I'll need a fully loaded iPad Air, with 128 gigs of RAM, Wi-Fi and a cellular connection. But sure, I can get you a version that works and show you how to operate it."

"I'll have a copy of the hard drive from the computer here tomorrow along with all the equipment you need."

Just then, the conference room door opened. Sam had barely enough time to turn around and stand up when Helen rushed over to him, nearly knocking him over with her embrace. Jamie hugged Pat as tight as she had ever held him.

"Don't ever leave me alone again?" she whispered in his ear.

"I won't." Pat responded between kisses.

"I'll leave you to get reacquainted. Come find me in the hangar when you want a ride home."

CHAPTER 41

SAM WAS SITTING IN THE LEATHER recliner in the family room. From his perch, he could look out the French doors into the backyard or watch television on the flat screen on the other side of the room. Tonight, all he wanted to do was stare out the window at the wooded property behind his house. He had poured a glass of Pinot Noir and one for Helen. Her recliner was empty for the moment. She was still in the shower upstairs. It had been far too long since she was clean. She needed to wash away the smell, the feel, every molecule that had contacted her over the course of the ordeal. It would take some time before things would get back to normal, before she would feel safe in her own home.

Sam's hand was shaking as he reached for his glass. Even now he could see the black barrel of the Makarov every time he closed his eyes. He knew how close he had come to death. Now somehow, he needed to bury that memory deep into the folds of his subconscious in a place where even he couldn't find it again.

It was a problem even he couldn't find a solution for. What he knew was that he could never, ever share the experience with anyone, least of all Helen. She had her own memories to deal with. He couldn't lay this one on her doorstep.

He flipped through the channels, turned the television off, picked up a book, and then put it back down again. He paced around the family room. Even the comfort of staring out the patio doors didn't offer relief. It would take time to recover.

* * *

Helen let the water wash down on her. She had turned the temperature up hotter than she typically set it. Somehow, she thought the water that was turning her skin red would burn the filthy memory off her. The water washed away the tears that flowed down her cheeks into her mouth. It would be ninety-seven minutes before she put on her robe and walked downstairs, the thinnest of smiles on her face.

Sam knew talking would be difficult. He wanted desperately to unburden himself, probably as much as Helen needed to. But it was not the best thing to do tonight, not the right thing to discuss tonight.

He finished his glass of wine, then poured another as he studied Helen's slender fingers twirl the glass as she stared blankly, not seeing anything in the room.

"Helen? I think we should take a vacation... to Paris."

THE END

ABOUT THE AUTHOR

W. M. J. Kreucher hails from the vibrant streets of west Detroit, a place that shaped his early years and ignited his passion for impactful change. With an illustrious career spanning over three decades, he delved deep into the heart of the automobile industry, carving a niche in the environmental sector. His dedication centered on championing clean fuels and enhancing vehicle fuel economy, lending his expertise to shape legislation and regulations. Not only did he craft compelling narratives as a ghostwriter for esteemed Congressmen and Senators, but he also played a pivotal role in shaping some of the very laws and regulations that govern our world.

Transitioning from the corridors of power, he has now embarked on a thrilling new chapter as a fiction writer. It's a departure from the scripted world of politics, a space where truth sometimes blurred with fiction. With a wry smile, he now calls it as he sees it, infusing his experiences into captivating stories that transport readers to worlds both familiar and extraordinary.

OTHER BOOKS BY THE AUTHOR

<u>DANDELION MAN</u> – THE FOUR LOVES

In the words of Sir James Matthew Barrie, "God gave us memory so that we might have roses in December.", and these roses inspire our protagonist to recount the story of his first love.

Growing up in the 60s was a unique experience, and our hero's coming of age story is unforgettable. According to the Midwest Book Review, 'Dandelion Man' is a must-read for those looking for a great work of general fiction.

Similarly, CatholicFiction.Net praises the story for being both compelling and engaging.

PHARMACEUTICAL

Greed, the Need for Power, and a Heroine

PHARMACEUTICAL is a gripping conspiracy thriller. The CEO, R. Curtis Larson, is a money-driven individual who doesn't hesitate to resort to unethical means to achieve his goals. Diane McMichael becomes an obstacle in his path, and both sides have influential allies that complicate the situation. If you crave an adrenaline-pumping novel that will keep you hooked until the very end, PHARMACEUTICAL is the book for you.

The audio book is narrated by noted actor and radio personality Samuel E Hoke. Mr. Hoke is a seasoned actor and voice professional. He has both radio and national television credits including twelve years of major market radio experience and hundreds of commercial audio productions.

HEAVEN SENT
Friendship; Loss; Love

HEAVEN SENT is a heartwarming coming-of-age tale set in the woods of Northern Michigan.

The story follows a young boy who spends his summer with his grandfather in Topinabee, and learns some valuable life lessons along the way.

This charming story is a perfect blend of sass, humor, and emotion. Whether you're looking for a poignant read or a delightful adventure, HEAVEN SENT is the book for you. So why not pick up a copy today and discover the magic of this wonderful tale?

THE INN AT HERON'S BAY

What's on your bucket list?

Discover the challenges faced by Elizabeth as she attempts to convert her family's old home and lighthouse into The Inn at Heron's Bay, located in the small town of Topsail in North Carolina, just south of the Outer Banks. When Dixon and Kathy arrive from the West Coast to study the area's beauty and history, they are in for a surprise. W. M. J. Kreucher's latest novella is a moving story set in a stunning location. If you enjoy a poignant story that highlights a beautiful area, then you will love this book. Purchase THE INN AT HERON'S BAY and start planning your own bucket list.

The audiobook is narrated by Ann Bumbak (www.seahorseaudio.com). Ann is a gifted voice actor having narrated more than a dozen audio books. She is also a prolific author. Her "Officer Down" series examining line-of-duty deaths due to firearms has achieved international recognition. Listen as Ann Bumbak brings the characters to life.

DRONE

DRONE is a captivating thriller that hooks you from the start and keeps you engaged till the end. It all begins with an innocent tweet, but things quickly spiral out of control when a rogue KGB agent named Vasili Grigory Konstantinov enters the picture. While Sam and Pat are happily in love with their significant others, Vasili has no attachments and only one purpose in life.

If you enjoy fast-paced stories, masterful storytelling, and unique protagonists, then DRONE by W. M. J. Kreucher is the perfect book for you. This prequel to AMIE will leave you on the edge of your seat and craving for more.

Narrated by the talented actor and radio personality, Samuel E Hoke, the audio version of

DRONE is a must-listen. With years of experience in the entertainment industry, Hoke brings the characters and the story to life in an unforgettable way.

AMIE

"Revenge is a dish best served cold." Devastated by the loss of Vasili Grigoriy Konstantinov, his beloved protégé who he saw as a son, Dmitri is determined to uncover the truth, and he knows that only Sam Kennedy can provide the answers he seeks. Discover the thrilling conclusion to the DRONE saga by purchasing AMIE today.

Two for Vengeance—The Kennedy Chronicles

"Two for Vengeance" narrates the story of Sam Kennedy, an ordinary man who gets involved in international intrigue. The first installment, "DRONE," portrays how this IT consultant got caught up in a terrorist attack on American soil. According to Newton's third law, every action has an equal and opposite reaction. "AMIE" explores the aftermath of the "DRONE" incident on Sam Kennedy's life.

POLONIA—PANI DEWICKA AND OTHER STORIES

Polonia narrates the story of Pani Dewicka and her descendants, who represent those who have suffered under oppressive regimes that have invaded foreign lands. The story spans across generations, chronicling the challenges faced by an ethnic family that ultimately migrates to the United States. While the tale references actual locations, individuals, and incidents, it is a work of fiction, and certain real events have been altered or reimagined in the narrative. After all, as it is said, we were all once strangers in an unfamiliar place.

THE BLUE NUN

Discover how a seemingly ordinary peasant from India, Dhanishta Goswami, and her daughter Khaliqa, become the central figure in a global terrorist incident in the book, THE BLUE NUN.

Uncover the intriguing story of their upbringing and the events that led to their involvement in the act of terror by purchasing a copy of this book.

WHILE DRIFTING SELECTED WORKS BY W. M. J. KREUCHER

Experience a journey from Topinabee to Topsail through the pages of **"WHILE DRIFTING,"** a collection of novels written by W. M. J. Kreucher. This captivating collection will take you through coming-of-age stories, romantic encounters, and a December-December love affair.

The collection begins with **"Dandelion Man— the four loves,"** the first story, which Mary Cowper from the Midwest Book Review called "enticing with a dedication to a very different era... well worth considering for general fiction collections." The Catholic Fiction website described the story as "both powerful and interesting." It is the first of "The McMichael Trilogy," with the lovable Diane McMichael as the protagonist.

The collection continues with **"Heaven Sent"** a heartwarming coming-of-age tale set in the woods of Northern Michigan. The story follows a young boy who spends his summer with his grandfather in Topinabee and learns some valuable life lessons along the way.

The third story, **"Pharmaceutical,"** offers a bit of political intrigue and a good conspiracy theory, according to Karen Kelly Boyce, the 2012 recipient of the Eric Hoffer Gold Award in Fiction. Boyce also said about the author, "...we may have a Catholic 'Robin Cook'."

The collection continues with **"The Inn at Heron's Bay,"** a novella set in coastal North Carolina in a small town with the delightfully descriptive name of Topsail.

The last part of the journey, **"Roses in December"**, is a poignant story of a man with Alzheimer's and his companion.

Join us on this captivating journey through **"WHILE DRIFTING."**

THE CURIOUS CASE OF THE BREVARD RECLUSE

In the serene town of Brevard, Sally Fowler's ordinary childhood takes a sharp turn when she stumbles upon the lifeless body of an elderly recluse while playing near the local pickleball court. Officer David Chapman, navigating the peculiar circumstances surrounding the recluse's death, uncovers clues that upend the initial assumption of a heart attack followed by a bear encounter. As the police delve deeper, a tale of hidden riches and tangled secrets unfolds.

Amidst the whispers and speculations, the Tuesday Night Book Club, inspired by their love for Agatha Christie's mysteries, emerges as unexpected sleuths in unraveling the enigma. Led by Mary, an elderly spinster with a penchant for astute observations, the club members delve into the recluse's past, piecing together a narrative that spans war, love, and betrayal.

While the recluse remains shrouded in mystery, his life story becomes a captivating puzzle for the book club members, each revelation propelling them further into the heart of Brevard's hidden history. Sally's innocent discovery becomes a catalyst, leading the book club on a thrilling journey through a web of secrets, bringing them closer to the truth buried beneath layers of deception and intrigue.